# OVERCOMING PREJUDICE

"Wake up, son of a Tartar dog!" These words resounded in Vaylance's skull, and a booted foot prodded him in the gut. Vaylance sat up. With a sickening feeling, he saw that it was getting dark. He'd overslept and missed his chance to enter the fort in daylight.

An enormous Cossack grinned down at him over rows of cartridge cases across his breast, a toothy snarl showing beneath a wheat-straw mustache. His blue eyes hungered like waiting vultures.

"Get a rope on him, Ivan Ivanovitch," he bellowed. "We'll teach this Muslim to drink vodka like a proper Christian before we cut his balls off!"

A rope fell in a tangled skein on Vaylance's legs.

"Hold off, Stepan. Don't mess him up too much," said Ivanovitch from his horse. "Maybe he's from one of the peaceful tribes. He has the look of the steppe about him. Not like those mountain devils we're after. . . . What's your tribe, boy?" Ivan Ivanovitch looked older than Stepan. On the lean side, he wore his black moustache curved like a Turkish scimitar.

"I'm Nogai," said Vaylance, trying to look as peaceable as he could. He wanted to conceal his Varkela origin from them, for the Cossacks had superstitions about the people who came out at night and drank human blood.

# Gifts Of Blood

## Susan Petrey

# GIFTS OF BLOOD

A Baen Book

Baen Publishing Enterprises
P.O. Box 1403
Riverdale, N.Y. 10471

ISBN: 0-671-72107-0

Cover art by Tim Hildebrandt

First Baen printing, February 1992

Distributed by
SIMON & SCHUSTER
1230 Avenue of the Americas
New York, N.Y. 10020

Printed in the United States of America

All proceeds from the sale of this volume will be donated to the Susan C. Petrey Clarion Scholarship Fund which assists new writers to attend both the Clarion and Clarion West Science Fiction Writer's Workshop.

A hardcover, limited edition book, *Gifts of Blood*, which contains these stories is also available from the following address:

Susan C. Petrey Clarion Scholarship Fund
P.O. Box 5703
Portland, OR 97228

The Fund is sponsored by Oregon Science Fiction Conventions Inc. (OSFCI), a non-profit tax exempt organization, and is presently administered by Debbie Cross & Paul M. Wrigley.

# ACKNOWLEDGMENTS

We would like to thank:

Phil Jansen, John Lorentz, David Johnson, and especially Marc Wells for the typing of the stories.

Steven C. Berry for turning the raw text into the finished book.

Sue's family for allowing us to publish the stories.

Ed Ferman for buying the stories in the first place, and Steve Perry for turning the unpublished rough manuscripts into stories.

The Directors of Clarion & Clarion West who have helped us in awarding the Scholarship each year.

The Portland Science Fiction Society and Oregon Science Fiction Conventions Inc., who have sponsored the Scholarship over the past ten years.

Westercon 43 and Oregon Science Fiction Conventions Inc. whose donation of funds has made the publication of this book possible.

And finally, all the people who have made donations to, or bought items at, the Susan C. Petrey Clarion Scholarship Auction.

# TABLE OF CONTENTS

# INTRODUCTION

## by Debbie Cross
## and Paul M. Wrigley

THIS BOOK EXISTS as a tribute to a gifted woman who died too young. Who was this Sue Petrey person anyway? She was a writer. She was a musician. She was a student of Turkish and Russian. She worked as a medical technologist. She was an early member of the Portland Science Fiction Society. She was a member of The Science Fiction Writers of America. Most of all, she was a friend.

Susan Candace Petrey, like many of us, was confused about her life. Her diary and doodlings revealed this. But she sought counseling from her church, from professionals, and from her friends. She lived her life, no matter how confused, with direction and intent. Much of Sue's energy was funneled into the study of languages and history. Many of her notes and story ideas were written in Turkish and Russian. She used this knowledge extensively in her writing, and it is evident in most of the stories in this book. She began writing as a means of combating depression, but it became much more. Her dedication to it was unquestionable. Although she never made it to Clarion Science Fiction Writer's Workshop because of financial problems, she did attend the Silver Lake Writer's Conference and was a regular at local informal writer's groups. Her efforts were rewarded when her first story was published in the September of 1979.

1

We only knew Sue for a few years and don't have much knowledge of her earlier life. There was a failed marriage, of which she spoke very little. We believe she grew up around horses. Her love of them is reflected in the golden-eyes mare of the Varkela stories. She loved all kinds of animals. Her favorite pet was a boa constrictor named Baby. Susan had a degree in microbiology and worked as a medical technician. Again, medical and healing themes occur throughout her writing. Another talent and love of Sue's was music. She was an accomplished mandolin player and often jammed with folk musicians in the Portland area. In spite of all of this, much of her life outside of her writing and science fiction fandom will remain unknown to us.

Sadly, Sue's life ended on December 5, 1980, at the age of 35. Her roommate found her at home, dead of an overdose of multiple substances. It has often been reported that she committed suicide. Mostly, we have refrained from discussing, in print, the circumstance of her death. But now, after so much time has passed, it no longer seems that avoiding the subject is the considerate thing to do. We know Sue was taking prescription tranquilizers, she had a cold and was taking cough medicine with codeine, and she had been drinking. No suicide note was found. Only earlier the same week she had received the letter accepting her fourth story for publication. She was very upbeat about this, finally admitting she was a professional writer. There is no way of knowing what really happened, but many of her friends who knew her well, and those of us who had been with her in the days just before her death, do not believe Sue took her own life. We prefer to believe that Sue would be with us today except for a fatal error in judgment—the mixing of the wrong drugs.

Sue left behind many friends and family who even now are saddened by her absence.

Why, so long after Sue's death, is this book finally

being published? For nearly eleven years we have organized and administered the Susan C. Petrey Clarion Scholarship fund, under the auspices of Oregon Science Fiction Conventions, Inc. Although the scholarship was meant to be a memorial to her, we found that few people remembered Sue, or had even read her stories. In 1990, we produced a limited edition book, *Gifts of Blood,* as a means of keeping her memory alive. Baen Books showed the good taste to make these stories widely available in paperback. Therefore, this book becomes a double tribute, both as a revival of her work and because all royalties go to support the scholarship in her name.

As mentioned earlier, four of the stories in this book had been accepted by Ed Ferman of *The Magazine of Fantasy and Science Fiction* before her death. Shortly after her death, Sue's roommate asked us to deal with all of Sue's notes, manuscripts, and other papers. Out of these, we found a number of uncompleted story ideas and some rough manuscripts. We asked Steve Perry, an already accomplished writer, if he could help in preparing what was usable for sale. Thanks to his efforts as "agent" three more stories were accepted posthumously. This book contains all of Sue's completed stories with one possible exception. We believe that a story about germ warfare was published in an obscure medical magazine. Unfortunately, it could not be located for inclusion here.

The first seven stories all exist in the same universe. One where non-human Varkela offer healing in exchange for small quantities of the blood they need to sustain life. You will find this to be a very refreshing divergence from the traditional blood-sucking vampire stories.

"The Neisserian Invasion" is a complete departure from the Varkela. In fact, some readers may even find this story about extraterrestrial veneral disease offensive. Certainly, some editors did, and so it is the only story which has never before been published. But it is ten years later and audiences are surely sophisticated enough for such a topic.

Finally, "Spidersong," is the story which earned Sue the nomination for a Hugo for Best Short Story and for the John W. Campbell award for best new writer. This musical fantasy may be her best story, or perhaps it is just the departure from the world of the Varkela that makes it seem so special. Either way we hope you enjoy this book, and by doing so, honor the memory of our friend Susan C. Petrey.

# SPAREEN AMONG
# THE TARTARS

WHEN THE TARTAR herdsman came to pay him, Spareen the Varkela was sitting before the fire outside his tent, chopping root of Valerian to make one of his medicinal infusions. Evening darkened the east, but the western sky still held a hint of sunset. He watched as the Tartar, with baggy trousers flapping in the wind, approached on horseback over the short grass of the Russian steppe.

I hope they've sent a healthy one, he thought, and I hope this payment will be enough for me this month. But he knew that it wouldn't.

"I've come to pay you for the healing of one of my kinfolk," said the dark-skinned Tartar, dismounting and tying his horse to a tent stake.

Spareen smiled carefully, hiding his partially retracted teeth behind closed lips. But for his teeth, he looked human. He noticed that the Tartar eyed him nervously. They always feared him, though he was only one among so many of them.

"Don't worry," said Spareen. "We never take too much."

He led the man into the tent and motioned him to sit on the Turkish rug. Then he began to sing softly in the old tongue, as he usually did before taking his rightful fee. The glazed expression in the Tartar's eyes told him his song was effective. He rolled up the sleeve of the man's musty tunic and felt for veins with probing fingers. When he found the proper vein, he placed his mouth to it. His thin, hollow blood-teeth punctured the skin and drew sustenance into his blood-starved vessels.

He counted silently as the warmth flowed into him, and when he had reached the proper number for a scant half-cupful, he withdrew his teeth and licked at the small punctures with his pink doglike tongue.

"A little will suffice for now," he thought. "It never pays to be greedy." He clapped his hands and the Tartar came out of the trance.

"You've paid," said Spareen. "You can go home now."

"So quickly?" exclaimed the Tartar, owl-eyed. "And it didn't even hurt at all." He followed Spareen out of the tent and untied his horse, which was tugging vigorously at a clump of yellow lady's-bed-straw.

As he watched the Tartar ride away into the rolling hills of the steppe, Spareen could still feel the pain of unsatisfied need, and it worried him. A small quantity, approximately two pints per month, was necessary to his survival, but he was new in this territory and finding subscribers to his medical services had been difficult. He had had an easy time of it, living with his father, who had a thriving practice among the Kalmuck nomads.

"Well, I suppose now I shall have to go out and hunt up a little vet work to make ends meet," he said and ducked back into the tent to gather up his saddle and his herbs.

Spareen could cure a horse of lameness in one day, his big fingers massaging blood into bruised joints or applying a strong-smelling poultice to a damaged fetlock. His healing touch worked better on animals than on humans. When the nomads of the steppe needed a Varkela leechman to cure the ague, or a toothache, they went to his father, Freneer, the shaman, or to his brother, Vaylance; but if it were a horse that was ailing, they would take extra effort to hunt up Spareen.

He was not always easy to find. He stayed at Freneer's yurt when he was on speaking terms with his father; and when he was not, which was often, he stayed with a Circassian woman in the mountains, a Nogai Tartar woman on the steppe, or sometime by himself, with only his little tent, just he and the golden-eyes mare, grazing, while he slept his deathlike sleep in the daylight hours.

Like all *Children of the Night,* he spoke the language of horses, but Spareen had taken the time to learn to speak to other animals as well and could summon the otter, Samuru, his soul-beast, from its lair along the Volga into the opening of his shirt, where it would drape itself like a fur collar.

His singing voice ran deep and clean, like the tolling of the larger church bell in the Cossack village. One could listen for hours as he sang the chant for his shaman father or some ribald Russian drinking song in a tavern.

Had anyone called him a Vampire, he would have shrugged his broad shoulders and said, "But Vampires are dead people, and I am not dead." He was pure Varkela of the old type, having thin, hollow blood-teeth where men of humankind have incisors, the so-called canine teeth, which in the Varkela were more fine and catlike. By the practice of medicine on man and beast, he earned the special sustenance these teeth demanded. He was careful to keep his teeth retracted around the Russians he dealt with. People who came out at night and drank human blood were viewed with suspicion by the Slavs, but the Tartars and Kalmuck nomads of the steppe welcomed these practitioners of leechcraft and came monthly to pay the *blood-price* for services rendered.

Payment had been skimpy for Spareen this month, and he knew that he must earn more before the dark of the moon, the "Blood Moon" as his people called it, the time when hunger became madness. Fortunately he had a call to make tonight; Yusef Bey had an ailing stallion and Spareen, if he effected a cure, would be well paid.

Dragging his saddle from the tent, he whistled sharply and the golden-eyes mare came and stood patiently as he tightened the girth around her sleek black belly and eased the bit between her teeth. Next came the saddle bags containing his pharmacopoeia of herbs, his small lancet of German steel, and two needles.

"Well, is it drinking or working tonight?" asked the mare in the horse language that only the Varkela understand.

"Working tonight," said Spareen, patting his fat saddlebags.

"And drinking on the morrow?" asked the mare.

"Perhaps," said Spareen, and as an afterthought, he reached into the tent again and slung his goatskin wine flask over his saddle bow.

"You drink too much, Spareen," said the mare.

"You think so?" asked Spareen. "I had not noticed."

"You should marry, Spareen," said the mare.

"Oho! So that's what this conversation is about," said Spareen, and prepared himself for a lecture.

"You drink too much lately because you are unsatisfied

with life. You should get you a wife and some children," said the mare.

"You know that I've been trying," said Spareen, "but the lady in question must also agree, and I have not heard from her these four days."

"If she keeps you waiting, propose to another," said the mare.

Finding a wife was not such an easy task for Spareen as the golden-eyes mare seemed to think, for to do this, he would have to find a woman of his own race, and Varkela women had always been rare, due to a sickness that claimed many of them before puberty. Because of this, Varkela marriages were polyandrous unions lasting only a few years until children were produced. Then the father departed with his offspring to instruct them in the healing arts.

As Freneer, his father, had told him, "Life is lonely without children to teach, and who will keep our knowledge alive if we do not produce children? For we are an old race and are dying out."

And so Spareen yearned after a "wolf-minded" girl, one of his own kind, like Varkura. Now there was a real woman! Not like the outblood women who became mute automatons when he witched them with his dark Varkela eyes. Varkura was defiantly an equal, a wolf-minded girl whose devil-dark eyes resisted the summoning power of his own.

At 32, she had already had several husbands, and she professed to being tired of one of the two she had now— she didn't say which—and that had raised his hopes. It was not her beauty that quickened his blood—although she had coils of long black hair, a straight Circassian nose and eyes as deep and still as the Volga on a summer's night. It was her scent that stirred the roots of his belly fur, calling to mind the Varkela saying, "A wolf-minded girl is friendly to the nose." It reminded him of wild ginger that creeps close to the floor of forested Caucasian ravines. Compared with her, all outblood women smelled flat and slightly rancid.

And so with pleasant thoughts of her in mind, Spareen vaulted into the saddle and set off on his night's work. The golden-eyes mare chose not to disturb his reverie and cantered evenly across the gently rolling steppe, until they reached the Blackwater Slough, a small tributary of the Terek where Yusef Bey, the Tartar prince, bred his fine horses.

The stars sprinkled a fine dust across the night sky as Spareen and his dainty mount entered the Tartar village. They passed the tall wooden tower of the minaret and several low one-story dwellings before turning in at the gate of Yusef Bey. Spareen tethered the mare to the fence and walked around the house to the horse pens, where he saw the light of an oil lamp glowing feebly. In the shadow stood Yusef Bey, the stocky, bearded Tartar chieftain, his brown skin creased like the shell of a walnut; and next to him stood a young man, richly attired in a tunic of black Circassian wool, bound at the waist with a red silk sash. A double row of cartridge cases adorned his breast. Spareen judged the man to be a Cossack from one of the Russian outposts along the river.

"Ho, Spareen!" called Yusef Bey. "Now I've got two doctor-men, for one of my sons rode over to the fort and brought back this fellow."

The Cossack raised a disdainful eyebrow toward Spareen's large frame and said, "It's a good thing they've called in someone with a bit of muscle. The way that horse is carrying on, it may require both of us to hold him."

Spareen resented the presence of this sneering Cossack, who seemed to imply that he was good for nothing but muscle; he felt insulted that Yusef Bey had called in an outsider. He was about to decline this case and leave, when an angry neigh reverberated from the stable, followed by loud, hollow pounding of hooves against wood. He then realized that his patient needed him, and he resolved to set aside his anger of the moment.

"He seems to be in quite a rage," said Spareen. "Let me talk to him."

"I'd advise you not to go in there," said the Cossack. "That horse is mad with pain and won't let me touch him."

"Come and watch, Cossack," said Spareen. "You may learn something." He strode confidently into the stable, welcoming the friendly smells of hay and manure, but as he approached the stall where the thick-necked stallion tossed its mane, he became aware of a peculiar odor that caused an uneasy feeling in the pit of his stomach. A thought tugged at his mind, but it was driven out when the large horse screamed in fury and threw its huge body against the rails. The wooden slats creaked and bulged as the horse bounced back off the boards and stood glaring at them through rheumy slits of eyes; foam drooled from the slackened lips as the horse heaved great gusts of air like a bellows. One foreleg bled where a gash had laid it open.

"I don't like his looks," said the Cossack. "I've treated horses in much worse shape than that, but I've never seen one driven to such a state of madness, even in the throes of colic."

"I agree with you," said Spareen. "He even smells wrong."

"I don't smell anything," said the Cossack.

"Outbloods never smell anything," said Spareen. "Can't even smell their own mother until she's been dead for three days."

"I'm not paying you two to stand around insulting each other," said Yusef Bey. He drew himself up to his not very imposing full height, his stomach bulging through his tunic.

"I don't know," mused the Cossack. "We could get ropes and throw him. That way we could do something about that leg."

Spareen spoke to the horse in the old language and received a snort for an answer. "I'd advise against it," he said. "He asks us to stay away from him. And there is something about that strange smell. It reminds me of something."

Spareen tried to remember where he had smelled such a strange odor of fear and frenzy before. Something tickled the back of his mind just out of reach.

"How long has he been this way?" he asked Yusef Bey.

"Since he shied and fell under me two days ago," answered the Tartar.

"Anything out of the ordinary before that?"

"Well, now that you mention it, he savaged a mare a few days ago, and he usually takes them without any fuss. He's been rather irritable all week. Wait—there is one thing. My son, Ali, was riding him about two weeks ago, when a bobac came running out of its hole and fastened on his leg. Ali had to dismount and beat it off with a stick. It was very strange. A bobac is such a small thing to be attacking a horse," said Yusef Bey.

Spareen puzzled over the reasons why a small earth-dwelling rodent might bite a horse. And then he remembered.

"When I was quite young, my father tried to treat a horse that had been bitten by a rabid wolf. We had to tie him down with stout ropes before we could kill him, and even then, he chewed through the wooden post that we had tied him to. The teeth marks were full of blood and foam. Your stallion smells the same as that horse did."

"Will you have to kill my stallion, then?" asked Yusef Bey.

"I am afraid so," said Spareen. "Otherwise, he might bite someone and pass the sickness on to them."

"You really think this horse has the mad dog's disease?" asked the Cossack doctor. "I myself have never seen it in a horse. And I'm skeptical about sense of smell as a basis for diagnosis. I'm inclined to think he has eaten some hemp and that accounts for his strange behavior."

"Perhaps you're right," said Yusef Bey. "I would hate to lose such a valuable horse over a mouthful of hemp. How sure are you, Spareen?"

"Surer than sure," said Spareen. "The nose remembers what the mind forgets."

The stallion, which had been standing quietly for the last few minutes, made a plaintive nicker and shook his mane.

"You see," said Spareen. "He wishes us to kill him before the madness overtakes him again. He wishes not to hurt those who love him."

Spareen said something to the horse. It raised its head and looked him in the eyes, then lowered its muzzle to the floor dejectedly.

"I can't let you kill him until I am sure," said Yusef Bey. "If it is hemp, it will be out of his system by tomorrow. And if not, I can put him out of his misery myself."

"No," said Spareen, "your horse is a noble fellow. I only wish I had met him under happier circumstances. I will come tomorrow and do the deed as it should be done. I will say the horse prayer over him, that he may find his way to the pastures of the spirit world." He hastened to add, "There is no charge for it."

"I'll come back tomorrow myself," the Cossack said. "You'll see that I'm right. I was educated in St. Petersburg, and I know a bit more than your witch-man from the steppes."

"I only wish you were right," said Spareen. The death of a horse always saddened him. Among the Varkela, horses were treated as kin and were addressed as "sister," "brother," or "spouse."

As there was nothing more to be done for the stallion that night, Spareen took his leave of Yusef Bey and rode back to his camp. On the way, he took several swigs from his wine flask and tried to ignore the gnawing hunger that pained his blood-teeth. Not to be paid was a serious problem this late in the month. He thought of Culeer, who had died several years back, when the Nogai Tartars refused to pay him the *blood-price*. Such a fate did not appeal to him.

There are other alternatives, thought Spareen, who did not always earn his blood by honest leechcraft but sometimes made the trade for love among the outblood people. This was frowned on by his father, who said, "Our own women will reject you if you continue in that way." Spareen seriously considered going to the fort village, which was not far away, and luring one of those handsome Cossack women out into the night. But then he thought of Varkura and decided against it for the time being.

He rode to the top of a small rise and was just about to turn toward his camp when he saw the light of a campfire in the opposite direction. He decided that he had better check out his new neighbors and gave the golden-eyes mare a nudge with his boot. She descended the grassy slope at a trot, and soon Spareen could see, rising from the dark steppe, the white mushroomlike forms of yurts, the homes of nomad people. It was a settlement of Kalmucks.

What luck! he thought. Surely someone here will require my services. And he set out to find the head man.

Dismounting before the most prominent yurt, with a

banner in front of its doorway, Spareen dropped the reins
and left the mare to graze.

"Does anyone here require healing?" he called out the
traditional question of his people.

A short swarthy Kalmuck came out through the door
flap and paused to look at Spareen, apparently sizing him
up before speaking.

"So, a Varkela," said the man. "We already have an
agreement with one of your kind, a fellow from across
the river."

That would be Culance, thought Spareen, and my luck
isn't changing as I'd hoped.

To the Kalmuck he said, "Is there no small healing I
could do here? For I have not earned enough this month
and I am fainting." He was not fainting yet, but it might
come to that.

The Kalmuck looked at him doubtfully and said, "Very
well, you may inquire of everyone here, but I'm afraid
you'll find us quite healthy—and, mind you, leave our
women alone."

Spareen went to the next yurt—there were only six in
all—and asked but found every family member free of
sickness. At the next, one child had a wart on his hand,
but they refused to let Spareen treat it, saying it would
go away on its own accord. And so it went, until Spareen
reached the last dwelling. There was a very pregnant
mare tethered outside this last yurt.

Well, thought Spareen, sometimes a man must make
his own luck. And he spoke to the mare, saying, "Lie
down little sister and don't get up until I tell you."

The mare knelt and rolled her ungainly form to one
side.

Spareen rattled the blanket at the door frame and said,
"It appears that you have a sick mare here. Perhaps I
can be of service."

An old woman came out and looked at the mare, lying

on the ground, and said, "By the Buddha's beard, she was fine just an hour ago. Perhaps she is dropping her foal now."

"I think not," said Spareen, "for there are no contractions and she's not breathing hard. I think it's a touch of the ague and that's especially dangerous when they are this close to foaling."

"Whatever shall I do? She's our best milk mare," said the woman.

"I think I can help her," said Spareen, "but you must be willing to pay my price."

"Yes, I know, you Varkela must have your price. My son will pay you. He's young and healthy. Do what you can for my mare."

So Spareen set about making his bogus cure. He spent a long time looking for a certain herb and then made a steaming infusion of this plant over the cookfire. After it had cooled, he placed a bowl of it near the head of the "sick" mare and helped her drink some of the harmless broth. Rather than profane the "chant of healing," he sang a folk song over the mare as he walked around her three times. He sang in Varkela, which the woman did not understand, about a young ruffian who wasted all his energy on drinking and outblood women and never got himself children. And then, because he felt a bit guilty, he got his hasp out of his saddlebags and filed his patient's hooves down, for they had been long neglected and had grown out to the point that it was difficult for her to go at a pace faster than a walk. In about an hour's time, the cure was successful and the mare scrambled to her feet when he gave her the command.

"Simply amazing!" said the woman. "One would never guess that an hour ago she was at the gates of death." She went off to fetch her son and shortly returned with a solid man of 35, smoking tobacco in a little silver pipe. Spareen led the man around to the back of the yurt and bled him from the arm for the allotted time. It wasn't much. His teeth cried for more, but he withdrew his mouth and found that they didn't hurt quite as much as before.

He went to find the golden-eyes mare. She had wandered off to graze, dragging her bridle reins along the ground. He found her among the nomad cattle, eating her fill of the scrubby grasses.

He gathered up the reins and prepared to mount her but before he could get his foot into the stirrup, she reached around and nipped him on the rump.

"Ow, now what's that all about?" he asked.

"Spareen, for shame!" said the golden-eyes mare.

"Well, she did need to have her feet trimmed," said Spareen, and he mounted and started for home. When he got back to his small camp, he noted by the stars that it was a little after midnight. He unsaddled the mare and rubbed and scratched her where the saddle had flattened the hair. Then he got his currying tools from the tent and began to ruffle the hair against the grain and then comb it out straight.

In the distance he observed a rider approaching that looked like Varkura. When he saw indeed it was she, he went walking out to greet her. He hoped that she had decided in his favor and would invite him to live with her, bear him children, to share his lonely life and instruct in the old tradition.

As she approached, he saw no smile of welcome on her face but, rather, a brooding serious look, as though she faced an unpleasant duty. He caught her horse by the bridle and stood waiting for her to speak. In answer to his unspoken question, she took from her embroidered waistband the little dagger he had given her in pledge and threw it down.

"Take back your own, Spareen," she said, her white blood-teeth winking in the corners of her mouth. Spareen bent to retrieve the dagger where it had stuck in the turf. His hand closed over the ivory hilt with its silver filigree.

"I take it that you refuse me then," he said. "But would you at least tell me the reason?"

"I have heard that you have polluted yourself over-much with outblood women. Perhaps you even have 'the house disease,' " she said. The "house disease" was what the yurt-dwelling peoples of the steppe called syphilis.

"I do not deny that I have been with outblood women. Who hasn't? I'll wager none of your husbands came to you a virgin. But I am not unclean. Do not reject me on that account," he said.

But she ignored his words, reined in her gray stallion and rode off into the night, her back straight as a knife blade, her long black hair flapping in the wind. Spareen stared down at his little dagger, a gift from the outlaw, Yurgi Khan, whose leg he'd sewn up after a skirmish with the Cossacks.

"If my luck continues like this," he said, "I ought to go down to the Turkish border, geld myself and enter a harem." He walked back to his tent, took up his curry comb and began to groom the golden-eyes mare again. She munched grass contentedly and did not offer any advice, for which he was grateful.

He realized that it was quite late. Around this time of night he was in the habit of taking his flintlock out and bagging a few large Russian hares for the supper pot. But although his belly was empty, he felt very little of that sort of hunger. His hollow veins craved other nourishment, and he envied humankind who never have that dark hunger, whose plump flesh was always full of the juice of life.

♦ ♦ ♦

The birds awoke long before dawn and began their morning chorus. Spareen, who often sang with them, did not have the heart today and crawled into his tent early to start his daytime sleep. In their state of daytime estivation, the Varkela had sometimes been mistaken for the undead, the Nosferat, and for this reason, Spareen made his camp far from the camps of men, and the golden-eyes mare stood sentinel while he slept. In the dark interior of the tent, Spareen slowed his heart and his breathing and slept the sleep of his people.

When he awoke again, the sun had just gone down and a mist of red lay over the western horizon. He remembered his words to Yusef Bey and prepared to return there this night to carry out the grim task of killing the stallion as painlessly as possible. He thought of how the noble beast had spoken to him, asking to be put to death rather than bring harm to his master. The otter, Samuru, came and begged to be taken along. Spareen scratched his fur and placed him in the saddlebags. Next, he gathered up his equipment, saddled the golden-eyes mare and rode off in the direction of the Terek. He arrived at the Tartar village as the last light was dying on the horizon. Yusef Bey was waiting for him at the stable, oil lamp in hand and the Cossack veterinarian stood a little one side. The light played on the double row of cartridge cases across his breast.

A piercing neigh came from the stable, followed by much kicking and banging of hooves.

"It appears, Spareen, that you were right all along," said Yusef Bey.

The Cossack said nothing, but Spareen thought there was less of the haughty look than he had seen before.

The same loathsome smell permeated the stable. Spareen saw where the stallion had bitten through one of the wooden posts that held the hay rack. The big horse stood in the far corner, his flanks heaving, his muzzle resting on the ground. Suddenly he raised his head and shook it violently as if trying to dislodge some unseen demon that clung there. He reared and lunged into the wall, smashing his shoulder into the boards, then stood there shaking all over, his frightened eyes rolling so that the whites showed like boiled eggs.

Spareen spoke to the horse in the old language, saying "I am here, little brother."

The stallion slowly raised his head and looked at Spareen. The wildness went out of his eyes and was replaced by such a look of sorrow, that Spareen could not bear to let the poor animal suffer any more.

"That's the first calm he's shown all day," said Yusef Bey.

"It's only the calm between storms," said Spareen. "We must hurry before the madness strikes again. I will need a strong rope and you must help me. Quickly now!"

A stout rope was fetched by Yusef Bey, and Spareen made a halter out of one length. He entered the stall and knotted it over the stallion's fine head. With the remaining rope, Spareen hobbled the front legs on the back, so that the horse could walk quietly but could not thrash about. Then with Yusef Bey holding the front rope and the Cossack holding the rear, Spareen slowly led the stallion out of the stall. In the yard behind the stable was a small incline. Spareen positioned the horse so that his rear legs were at the top and his forelegs at the bottom of this hill.

"Lie down, little brother," he commanded. "It will be all over soon."

The horse obeyed, but as soon as he lay on his side on the ground, the madness seized him and he began tossing about, struggling against the ropes. With a deft movement, Spareen looped the rope in such a way as to bring the front and rear legs together and tied them fast. Then he walked around to the head, knelt down and put his knee on the stallion's great thick neck. He could feel the muscles flex and pull under him. With his little scalpel of German steel, he found the pulsing artery in the throat and made a quick incision. Blood flowed out of the wound in a thick river, downhill into the depression where it pooled. Spareen could feel the life oozing out from the great body. Slowly, the flexing subsided and he felt the neck go limp under his knee.

Spareen felt a song rise in his throat. He loosed his mighty voice and sang the horse prayer, as his people had sung it through the ages to ease the passage of their brothers to the spirit world.

When the horse had breathed its last, Spareen stood up and began to clean his scalpel on a bit of cloth he carried for that purpose. He tossed the rag down by the carcass and said to Yusef Bey:

"You must dispose of the body by burial and burn the ground where the blood has spilled. Be careful that no blood or saliva touch you."

"Why such superstitious ritual?" asked the Cossack doctor, whose 19th century education had taught him little of contagion.

"I do not know," said Spareen. "We have always treated certain diseases this way. It is the old knowledge."

They walked back to the barn. Spareen overheard the Cossack remark, "One might almost believe that old tale about those who speak the horses' language." The Cossack doctor mounted his horse and bade them good evening. Spareen gathered up his saddlebags and was preparing to leave, when Yusef Bey asked him to come in for a moment and have some refreshment.

"I cannot offer you the customary fee, as you have not healed," said Yusef Bey, "but your people do eat as other men, don't they? I have fresh cream butter, bread and cheese."

Spareen, who had not filled his stomach since the night before, accepted the hospitality and went into the house. At a small table lighted by a single oil lamp, he was offered little bread pockets of cheese and sweet cream butter by a buxom young woman.

"My daughter, Halima," said Yusef Bey, as the girl served them.

"Your daughter, the slave!" snapped the girl and spun on her heel and walked out of the room.

Spareen's gaze followed the retreating roundness of Halima, and he was reminded of the small Persian melons that overflow with sweetness in the summer market stalls.

"She's angry," said Yusef Bey, "that we've promised her in marriage to a rich man. I'll tell you a secret. She saw you last night and said to me, 'There is none handsomer than Spareen of the Varkela.' She favors you, Spareen, but I must ask you not to witch her."

Spareen, who had been thinking of doing just that, smiled sheepishly and stared at the tabletop. "All right," he said, "you have my promise." But a slight hint of a smile remained on his lips.

Yusef Bey was not satisfied. "What do you swear by?" he asked with some suspicion.

"By my father's blood," sighed Spareen, who regretted being bound by an oath, "by the great mother tree that upholds the world, and by the gray-ghost stag sacred to my people Varkela."

Thus reassured, Yusef Bey resumed his supper, tearing at the bread with his old yellow teeth. Halima had brought them soured milk to drink, and Spareen, true to his word, did not seek to engage her glance but thanked her politely with lowered eyes. When the meal was finished, he said farewell to Yusef Bey and went out into the night. The wind was fragrant with sweet grass scent, and the black sky was swept clear of clouds so that only the clean white stars remained.

Spareen was tightening the saddle girth against the

belly of the golden-eyes mare, when he heard the rustle of women's clothing behind him.

"You go back, then?" said Halima. The sleeve of her dress barely brushed his arm. Her perfume, mixed with the scent of warm flesh, caused his mouth to water involuntarily. The golden-eyes mare closed her nostrils to slits and stamped a hind foot.

"Yes, I'm leaving now," said Spareen, "and you'd better go back into the house. What would your father say if he knew you approached strange men in the dark?"

"I'd tell him you lured me out here and broke your promise," she said. "So you'd better be kind to me, hear me out."

"Apparently, I've no choice," said Spareen. Her bare throat, milky and smooth in the dim light, tempted him awfully, and he felt his thin blood-teeth begin to protrude beyond their normal, slight retracted position.

"Speak your say then," he said.

"I've heard how Varkura misused you, Spareen. I wanted to tell you I sympathized," she said.

"So, everyone knows about my love life," sighed Spareen.

"Word gets around on the steppe," she said.

"Well, are you going to give me advice?" he asked. "Everyone seems to be giving me advice lately."

"No," she answered and looked shyly down at her feet. She seemed to be deliberating over what she wanted to say. Finally, she blurted out, "I want to offer myself in her stead."

Spareen laughed gently and patted her shoulder. "Little one," he said, "we only marry among our own kind." He felt protective toward her, as she was not more than 18 years old. Her boldness reminded him of his first brash offer to a woman twice his age and how she'd laughed at him.

Halima stared at her feet a few moments to gather her

thoughts and then said, "You've taken women without marriage before. Take me with you. You are lonely and I've no desire to marry the fat old man my father has chosen for me."

"And when I leave you, what will become of you? Have you thought of that? Your parents would most likely sell you into slavery among the Turks. I would not want that on my conscience." He was about to send her away, when suddenly the stars spun dizzily overhead and the grass fell up and hit him in the face.

"What's the matter?" she asked, bending over him where he had fallen.

He raised his head feebly, and when that proved to be too great an effort, he rolled over on his back and looked up at her where she knelt over him.

"It's the blood need. I fainted."

"Father didn't pay you?" she asked. She lowered herself to his level, placing her neck close to his face. "Here, take from me."

"I have not healed. Therefore, I've not earned payment," he said. "And, besides, we do not take from the neck except in the act of love."

She was lying on the grass, looking down at him. When he made this last statement, her face brightened with a smile, and with a quick movement she placed her leg over his, as if she would slide over on top of him.

"No, you mustn't," he said, sitting up suddenly, almost bumping heads with her. "I've promised your father."

"You only promised not to witch me," she said. "I have come of my own free will."

Spareen pondered this a moment. Technically, she was right. But sadly he realized he was not equipped to take advantage of the situation, having not enough blood to sustain an erection. And the blood need gnawed at him, driving all other needs away, in its craving for thick red warmth.

"Oh, your teeth," she said. "They're getting longer."

She touched one of the fine, needlelike points where it protruded over his lower lip.

"Ow, now it's cut me," she said, holding her finger up to his mouth.

He healed the tiny wound with a lick of his thin dog-like tongue. A sly smile played over his features and he observed her through half-closed eyes. She shivered when his lips brushed her throat, at first timidly seeking, then eagerly nuzzling the right spot, licking, and then the love-bite. Life flowed into him in waves. One wave refreshed the dry river bed of his sexual desire and it swelled in a mighty flood. He withdrew his teeth and sealed the pinprick wounds with his tongue.

She played her hands across the front of his trousers. Her finger came to rest on a small damp spot.

"You're wet," she said, stroking the firmness under the drawstring of his pants.

Spareen judiciously chose his best line.

"He weeps," he said. "He wishes you to comfort him." And then he thought of Yusef Bey and hastened to add, "Of your own free will, of course."

"Of my own free will," she smiled down at him and then, shifting her weight strategically, she prepared to comfort him.

◆ ◆ ◆

He was rubbing comfrey leaves to the wound on her neck and abrading it gently with his fire-cleansed scalpel.

"You can say that you scratched yourself on a bramble," he said. "On your wedding night, put some blood on a sponge under the sheet so that your husband does not reject you."

"What if I should have child?" she asked.

"That seldom happens with outblood women," said

Spareen. "Still, if it should, send word to me and I'll
come for you."

"But I'll be married by then."

"I'll come for you, if the child is mine, but I've never
been that lucky in the past."

He helped her up from the grass where they had beat
it down. There was a small spot on his trousers where
she had shed maiden blood. He noted that she looked
at him hopefully but did not cling to him, and he felt
guilty that he could not love her. Still, he knew the situation demanded some show of tenderness, and he was
grateful for the strength that now flowed through him.

Reaching into one of his plump saddle pouches, he
found Samuru, the otter, curled and sleeping. He pulled
the otter out of its nest and offered it to Halima.

"You won't need to feed him," said Spareen. "He's a
night hunter. He takes of himself."

She cradled the smooth-haired otter in her arms.

"I'll think of him as your child," she said softly.

Spareen watched as she walked stealthily back to the
house and crept in the back way. The golden-eyes mare
laid her ears flat and reached around to bite him, but he
jumped just out of her reach, then bounded into the
saddle before she could collect herself for another try.

"Jealous, my love?" asked Spareen.

"You'll never make any children that way," said the
mare.

He nudged her sides and she set off in a lope. The
rolling steppe spread out before them like a furry quilt
in the starlight. The stars stretched in a milky haze across
the silent summer sky. A large Russian hare darted out
of a hillock, and crossed his path, but Spareen did not
feel like shooting tonight. A sadness was passing through
him now that all his needs were met, and the scent of
wild ginger seemed to hover just beyond his reach. When
they came to the crest of the hill and were looking down

on his little tent, Spareen nudged the mare the other way, toward the road to the Cossack village, for he'd just seen a vision of himself sitting in the tavern, his teeth fully retracted, singing the lonely night away, and his heart moved toward that vision.

"So, it's drinking again," said the golden-eyes mare.

"And singing," said Spareen.

"And being sick on the morrow?"

"Perhaps."

"You should marry, Spareen," said the golden-eyes mare.

"You've said that before," said Spareen.

# FLEAS

LATE SUMMER WAS flea season on the Russian steppe. Spareen awoke to find several of the small bedfellows nipping amid his belly fur.

"Ho! Little brothers, am I the first course or dessert?" he asked as he plucked them out one by one and threw them out of the tent.

"Don't throw them out here," said the golden-eyes mare. "They'll just get on me and I don't like them."

"I like them," said Spareen. "Like me, they need blood to survive. I know what it feels like to have that kind of hunger, and I don't begrudge them a few drops." Spareen's were-teeth stirred from their little niches in his upper jaw as hungry thoughts came to him.

"Sympathy toward fleas! Now I've heard everything!"

neighed the mare. "You should break them between your fingernails like the Cossacks or throw them into the fire like the Tartars. They cause disease, and as a Varkela leechman, you are pledged to fight against disease, are you not?"

"True," said Spareen. "But fleas cause disease only in association with rodents, and I am not a rodent. Therefore these are innocent fleas and I can like them if I choose. Like me they need blood, but like me they give something in return for the blood they take."

"Now I've heard everything," said the golden-eyes mare. "A Varkela leechman gives healing in return for the blood he takes. But what on Earth does a flea give?"

"Just one thing," answered Spareen. "When a flea bites you it makes an itch, does it not?"

"Yes," said the mare.

"And when you scratch an itch, it really feels good. So there you are."

"You still haven't convinced me," said the golden-eyes mare.

"We will have to agree to disagree on some things," said Spareen, and picking up his medicine bag he began to fill it with herbs to prepare for his night's work.

# THE HEALER'S TOUCH

"WE WILL NO longer pay you the *blood-price*," said the Nogai Tartar chieftain looking down at Vaylance from the back of his stumpy, ewe-necked horse. A whole tribe of these small, dark men had ridden over to tell him this. Wind whipped the Tartar's baggy horsemen's trousers and hissed through the tall feather grasses of the Russian steppe that barely brushed the horses' bellies.

Vaylance resisted an urge to wipe his nose on the cuff of his black Kalmuck jacket. At 16, he was shaman's apprentice and must maintain some show of decorum. Silently cursing the allergies that had plagued him since he came to the steppe, he chose his words carefully.

"We have always cured your ills in the past. Do not forsake us now."

The hawk-nosed Nogai continued to peer at Vaylance sternly from under his shaggy sheepskin hat.

"You have not healed; therefore, we will not pay," and so saying, turned his horse and rode back the way he had come, his followers harrowing a path through the tall grasses. The sun made an ocher wound on the western horizon where gauzy clouds moved to cover it.

Black-water fever was the cause of the Nogai's refusal to pay. Clouds of biting insects drifting up from the marshes and backwaters of the Volga brought with them the usual summer fevers, but this year malaria, the dread black-water disease, was taking a heavy toll, and Vaylance's father, the Varkela shaman, knew no herb or treatment specific for the disease.

Vaylance stood watching, pondering his situation. The Nogai's declaration came at a bad time, with his sister Rayorka sick and badly in need of blood-payment. He turned his back on the Nogais and ducked through the leather door of his father's yurt, a dwelling of thick felt stretched over an umbrella-like wooden frame. He finally wiped his recalcitrant nose on the sleeve of his black Tartar jacket—the last gift his mother had given to him when he had come here at age twelve, barely a frightened child, to take his apprenticeship as a Varkela shaman, leaving her to continue her practice as a medium and spiritual healer in the garret séances of Petersburg. She had sent him to his father to learn the ways of his people. "For you must never forget that you are Varkela," she had admonished him. On the steppe, life was much different, and at first he had resented the seemingly uncouth savage that was his father, until he had seen the shaman cure ills that the Petersburg doctors, with all their pills and powders, couldn't touch. It was then that his apprenticeship had really begun, as he grew to respect the healing methods of his people, an old race that called themselves Varkela, *The Children of the Night*.

In the darkness of the yurt Vaylance blinked a few times as his nocturnal eyes made the transition. His half-sister, Rayorka, 14, was lying on the Turkish carpet. She smiled wanly and beckoned him to come sit beside her. In her weakened state she could barely raise her head. His brother, Spareen, 11, small and stout with his hair tied back in a tail, was sitting along the far wall, polishing his saddle with a little soap and oil. The leather squeaked congenially under his ministrations, and the smell of leather and neat's-foot oil mingled pleasantly with the sweet scent of herbs that hung from the ceiling in bunches; vervain, sweet flag, chamomile, valerian root, and willow leaf.

"The Nogais have refused to pay us," he announced, kneeling down to sit on the rug. His retractable blood-teeth ached in his jaw from his hunger, and he wondered what Rayorka must be feeling, for her hunger would be twice his now that her menses had started. She certainly looked pale and tired. This was a dangerous time for a Varkela girl—few of them survived puberty to adulthood due to the insidious nature of the blood-need. She was a pretty one, dark-haired and dark-eyed like her two brothers. Breasts were just beginning to form buds beneath her smock. Vaylance counted himself lucky to have a sister—so many of the female children were stillborn. As he watched, she closed her eyes and dozed.

Spareen finished scrubbing the saddle and stood up to lug it outside, apparently ready to talk horse-talk with the herd.

"If she's going to be sick for a while, can I ride the sorrel mare?" he asked. That was Spareen for you, preferring horses to people.

"Our sister may die, and all you can think about is riding her horse. No wonder Father calls you the selfish one. Why don't you help me by making a fire and boiling up some willow-leaf tea?" Vaylance gestured toward the blackened kettle that hung on a rod over the fire pit.

"Make fire in here on such a hot night?" asked Spareen. "We'll roast her to death. Besides, willow-leaf tea won't help blood-need."

"Make the fire outside then," said Vaylance. "Willow tea will at least ease the pain in her joints."

"It seems like all we ever do is take care of her any more," said Spareen, sullenly, reaching for the flint and steel that hung on the yurt frame by the door. As a parting shot, he asked, "If she wakes up would you ask her about the mare?"

Vaylance was on his feet in an instant.

"Get moving, fart-maker!" He snatched one of the ceremonial antlers from his father's gear and attacked his brother's retreating rump, but Spareen, agile as his soul-beast, the otter, narrowly avoided the prongs and sprinted through the flap to safety.

Vaylance eased himself down and lay beside his sleeping sister. He reached into a pocket and drew a piece of cord and tied it around his upper arm, causing the veins to show in the crook of the elbow. Gently he shook her awake and pressed his naked arm to her lips.

"Here, Ray, take it from me."

"No, you need it." She pushed his arm away, but he insisted.

"I have enough, I was paid yesterday." He forced the arm to her mouth and this time she acquiesced. One of her thin, sharp were-teeth punctured the vein and his life blood flowed into her.

He had not always had a sister. He remembered the night, two years ago when the tall, severe Cossack woman had ridden into their camp with the slip of a girl mounted up behind.

"Take back your Satan's whelp, Freneer!" She had addressed his father.

"What do you mean, woman?" asked Freneer, standing up, running a wrinkled hand through his long gray hair, tied back with string.

The woman untied the girl's blouse strings, and ignoring her protest, peeled back the cloth to reveal her naked chest. In the slight groove between the unformed breasts grew a patch of gray down-like fur, which diffused into scant peach-fuzz over her belly.

"If I fathered a child, you might have told me, and I'd have gladly taken her," said Freneer.

"I had not known she was yours until now, when she began to grow hair like your kind. If I marry her off, her husband will scorn her and make her a laughing stock in the village."

"She will be highly prized among us," said Freneer. "A female of the blood is always welcome."

The woman remounted and rode away, leaving them to comfort as best they could the frightened new addition to their family. Freneer had christened her Rayorka, or "little treasure." Spareen had resented his father's new favorite, but Vaylance took her under his protection. He knew what it was like to be uprooted and replanted in a strange place. He spent much time helping her to adapt to her new life, and soon she knew how to gather the right herbs for medicine, how to speak the horse's language that only the Varkela understand, and how to take the payment for such services in human blood.

Vaylance could hear the crackling of brush outside the yurt as Spareen attempted to make a fire. He was watching a bead of moisture roll down the side of the waterskin that hung on the wall to drop onto his sister's hair, when Spareen called out to him:

"There's someone coming!"

Vaylance drew his spare, lean frame up from the rug

and ducked out the door flap. It was getting dark, but he could easily see that a distant speck approached across the billowing waves of grass. As the rider drew nearer Vaylance identified him as a Kalmuck by his high cheekbones, slanted oriental eyes, and the dark-colored knee-length jacket flapping in the wind. They were a nomadic people of Mongolian origin, of a later migration than the Nogais who touted themselves as descendants of Ghenghis Khan.

"I hope he's coming to pay," said Vaylance, feeling his mouth water in anticipation. The tips of his blood-teeth began to protrude from their little sheaths in his upper jaw. It had been a week since the last one had come, in spite of what he'd told Rayorka—and it was near time to feed their hunger again.

"He'll pay," said Spareen. "The Nogais may forsake us, but the Kalmucks have never let us down." He was poking at a pile of brush that generated more smoke than fire.

But the Kalmuck had not come to pay. He pulled his stocky little horse to a stop, dismounted, flipped his queue over his shoulder, and began to explain how he'd taken a fall in a marriage-day horse race and said, "Leechman, I believe that the arm is broken."

Vaylance drew back the wide sleeve of the man's jacket and saw that the arm was quite bruised. His probing fingers detected a fracture. There would be no payment from this one until he was healed up, Vaylance thought, as he led the man into the yurt, gathered a pair of splints and began to tear the linen they kept for bandaging. After half an hour of deft maneuvering, the bone break was set. Vaylance yearned to press his lips to the healthy arm and bleed payment into his aching vessels—but that just wasn't done, not until the patient was well enough to sustain the loss. He pressed a parcel of comfrey root into the Kalmuck's hand and explained how to make bone-set tea, before sending him on his way.

As the figure grew smaller in the distance, Vaylance could feel the pain of his unsatisfied need. It was at times like this that he envied Spareen, who would not know this dark hunger for another two years.

Two kepar a month, a little over a pint, was all that Vaylance needed, taken a little here, a little there, from those who subscribed to the medical services of his father. That was not difficult, for Freneer's reputation as a healer was well known on the steppe. But they had not figured on Rayorka's getting "the sickness," or on the Nogai's refusal to pay. Something would have to be done.

◆ ◆ ◆

Vaylance returned to Rayorka's side. He was just settling down on the worn carpet when Spareen stuck his head in the door and said, "The water boils."

"Take a cup and steep ten willow leaves," Vaylance ordered. It was an old pain remedy good for headaches and joint ailments. Spareen came in, reached overhead and began stripping dry leaves from the trailing willow branches. He grabbed one of the two tin cups that hung on pegs from the yurt frame and slipped out the door, returning quickly, clutching the steaming cup by the brim.

"By the blood, that's hot!" he exclaimed, blowing on his fingers, after setting it down.

"Let the tea cool while I try a different remedy," said Vaylance. Assuming a cross-legged position, he placed his hands so that his fingers touched in a steeple pose.

"I'm going to try healer's touch." This was one area where his people's methods far outshone the Russian physicians in Moscow.

"You're going to touch heal without Father here?" asked Spareen, incredulous.

"Yes, I've done it before without his help—remember how I healed the Cheremiss boy with brain fever?"

"But Father was there with you every minute of that. I saw you with your fingers fluxing one minute and dead the next. Father was just about to put up his hand and stop you, but somehow you managed the transition on your own."

"And I couldn't have done it at all without your proper singing of the chants," said Vaylance, who knew that Spareen's objection was based in part on envy. A touch-healer was greatly respected among the Varkela, and Vaylance had begun to show signs of this gift at an early age.

"Do you really think touch healing will help her?" said Spareen. "I thought it was only good for brain fever and diseases of the soul."

"Who knows if healer's touch works only on the soul?" said Vaylance. "Don't all diseases in some way or other affect the soul? Look at our sister there. Isn't her soul in pain as well as her body?"

Spareen looked at Rayorka. Her eyes wandered unseeing beneath translucent lids.

"Well . . . she does look as if her soul has strayed. . . ." he began.

"Then we shall call it back," said Vaylance. "We must at least try. She's getting weaker, and there's no telling when Father will get back. He would be pleased if we put some of our training to use."

"Or angry if we muff things up," said Spareen. "But there's no use arguing with *you* once your mind is made up on something. Do you want me to sing the words or just hum the tune?"

"With words of course."

"What if I say it wrong and a ghost comes?"

"Don't be silly," said Vaylance. "You've heard Father

say it a million times and sometimes even his tongue slips, but no ghost ever comes."

"I don't know," said Spareen. "Remember the old story of how the shaman Sarmance accidentally called up the Mother of Horses, and she made him sterile, saying, 'Thy seed shall have no issue'?"

"You're a bit young to be concerned about being sterile, Spareen."

"I don't want to take any chances," said Spareen. "When I grow up, I want to be able to get a child on an outblood woman, like Father."

Vaylance laughed at this statement. Matings with humankind were often unproductive, and to impregnate a human female was regarded as a sign of especial virility.

"I'm sure you will, Spareen, since you've exceptional talent for mischief, but there will be plenty of time for that. Now, let's get on with it, or I *shall* summon up a ghost to make *you* sterile."

◆ ◆ ◆

Thus admonished, Spareen began to sing the chant, his pure treble mingling with the cricket voices in the grass outside. Vaylance set his mind to the task. Since coming to the steppe, he had had to learn a whole other way of thinking. Pressing his fingertips lightly together and then drawing them apart, he began to feel the pulse and flow of energy across the gap. The flux was thin and tenuous as spider silk, spanning the distance between his fingers like elastic thread, stretching thin when he moved his hands apart, and becoming a faint blue haze as he brought them together, thickening the field.

He shifted his weight so that he could touch Rayorka's forehead with one hand. Her eyes opened and the blue aura of his fingertips shimmered in their dark depths, but she appeared not to see him. Spareen reached the

end of the stanza and began to croon the high, keening
sound that came between verses.

In a low voice, Vaylance spoke to the soul of his sister.
He willed the power in his fingers to reach into her skull
and placed a hand on her stomach to receive the flow as
it returned to him.

Rayorka stirred under his touch. She blinked her eyes
and said, "Vaylance, is it you? Your hand feels cool, and
I'm so hot."

Vaylance helped her sit up and placed the cup to her
lips, that she might drink the infusion. She drank slowly,
her hands shaking as she tried to hold the cup. Vaylance
steadied her until she got it all down.

"I had the strangest dream," she said. "There was a
little man mounted on the back of a gray stag. Ohhh—
he's calling to me. . . ."

"Don't listen to him, Rayorka, stay with us," Vaylance
implored her, but she slowly relaxed in his arms and was
lost to him again.

Vaylance knew that the gray-ghost stag was the guide
to the nether world, the soul-beast of the shaman. He'd
seen it himself when his father had given him ceremonial
hashish at his initiation, but to the noninitiate he knew
the stag implied approaching death.

Spareen began a new verse, chanting louder, as if he
hoped by singing to bring her back.

As he held her, Vaylance, in his deepening trance
state, saw a movement at his sister's nose. A small gray
head poked out of her left nostril. He watch as the tiny,
gray wolf, soul-beast of his sister, carefully sniffed the air
and proceeded to leave the cave of the nostril, wandering
down her lip, across her chest and finally descending to
the floor of the yurt. The little wolf paused to look back
at him once, poised there, one paw lifted, and then departed through a crack in the felt siding. Vaylance tried
to follow in his mind and found himself within a dark

tunnel. There was a dim light at the end and he could see the small wolf trotting a ways ahead. He tried to project himself in the same direction when, suddenly, a tall, gaunt red-eyed shape reared before him. A swirling fog thickened and coalesced into the thin, cadaverous gray-ghost stag, trailing mist like grave clothes.

"You must not pass," said the red-eyed stag. Small green fires played among its antlers and skeletal ribs showed under its taut hide.

"I must follow my sister," said Vaylance.

"Where she goes, you may not follow," said the stag. "She will stay with us until you've earned blood and life enough to sustain her. She will stay forever if you do not."

Then the image faded and Vaylance was next aware of someone calling his name. He opened his eyes and saw the stag again in hazy vision, blinked, and saw that the leathern ancient face of his father, Freneer, gazed at him from beneath the shaman's staghorn headdress. Freneer reached up and removed the "two trees of wisdom" from his head and placed them on the low altar made from a wooden box.

"Praise the moon," he said, his weathered features cracked with lines of care. "I was afraid that we had lost you to the eternal dream. You must never do that without my help. Not until you are firmly grounded."

Vaylance sat up and rubbed his eyes. His mouth tasted as if he had been long asleep. "How long have I been in trance?" he asked.

"I've been trying to wake you for two hours. Spareen says you were in trance before the moon went down."

"What of Rayorka?"

"She worsens. Spareen tells me the Nogais have refused to pay us. If this is true she will die, for without their support we cannot expect to nurse a woman

through 'the sickness.' We will be lucky to earn enough
to sustain you, my son."

"But if we found a cure to the black-water disease,
then they would pay us," said Vaylance.

"But there is no cure," said Freneer. "Neither touch
healing, nor herbs, nor diet, nor singing of the chant can
cure black-water fever."

"Still, there must be a way, and I intend to find it,"
said Vaylance. "I will go on a healer's quest. Perhaps
there is a Russian doctor at the Cossack fort at Groznoi
who knows of a cure."

"A Russian doctor? I've little use for them. Their way
of healing is to bleed patients nearly to death."

"Not all of them practice bleeding," said Vaylance.
"Some of them produce cures with powerful medicines.
Perhaps they have one for black-water fever."

"And how would you persuade this doctor to help you?
For if he be of Slavic race and finds out what you are,
he will drive a stake through your heart to 'save your
soul,' as their perverse religion teaches."

"They needn't find out what I am," said Vaylance. "I
will keep my blood-teeth retracted in their sheaths. Everyone will think I am just a Tartar from the steppes. I
will not tell them that I need the cure to earn blood."

"I can see that you are determined to go," said Freneer, and to Vaylance he seemed suddenly very old and
tired. Lines wrinkled his brow and then smoothed, as he
heaved a great sigh, as though setting down a heavy bur-
den. "We are an old race, and we are dying out," he
said. "I suppose it doesn't matter whether it happens
now or a little later. My blessing on you; may you stay
in the land of the living."

◆ ◆ ◆

Vaylance set out at daybreak, the time when Varkela
normally settled into their death-like daytime sleep. He

tied a piece of black cloth over his nocturnal eyes to protect them and turned Spurka, his little Turkmene mare, toward the South. On the way he told her of the importance of his mission, and she gave encouragement in the horse language, twitching an ear to say, "Don't worry, young master. I will travel quickly."

Her smooth, swinging trot ate the versts, and he began to see in the distance the abrupt blue wall of the Caucasus Mountains that terminated the vast grassy steppe. The armies of Czar Nicholas I were at war with the fanatic Moslems of the mountains and the fort at Groznoi was one of the chief military outposts in the area. For this reason, Vaylance had deemed it prudent to approach the fort in the daylight hours, that he might not be mistaken for an enemy. If he'd figured right, he would arrive in the late afternoon.

At midday he stopped, for he was feeling a little weak—probably the blood-need gnawing at his vitals, he thought—a brief rest wouldn't hurt anything. He poured himself a frothy bowl of kumiss from the goatskin bag over his saddle bow and lapped at it with his pink dog-like tongue. He was immediately reminded of Rayorka's funny little outblood tongue, no good at all for licking. Not two days ago her hands had milked the mare that had provided him this meal. A lump rose in his throat and he fought back tears—*little sister, who mended the steppe owl's broken wing, will I ever see you again?* He realized that he would need his wits undulled by emotion if he expected to carry out his mission. He pushed Rayorka from his mind and concentrated on the black-water fever. It was a painful disease that left the body racked and wasted between bouts of chills and fever. Discolored urine gave the disease its name and was the most serious stage of the illness. And its contagion was such that no Varkela leechman dared take his special wages until symptoms had been gone for several years. Payment was usually taken from healthy members of the family in these cases. Vaylance had savored the taste of his last payment like scarlet liquor on the tongue—a strapping Nogai with veins thick as stems of cattail. His blood-teeth ached at the thought as he allowed himself to drift in currents of sleep. Only a few minutes, he promised himself.

◆ ◆ ◆

"Wake up, son of a Tartar dog!" These words resounded in Vaylance's skull, and a booted foot prodded him in the gut. Vaylance sat up. With a sickening feeling, he saw that it was getting dark. He'd overslept and missed his chance to enter the fort in daylight.

An enormous Cossack grinned down at him over rows of cartridge cases across his breast, a toothy snarl showing beneath a wheat-straw mustache. His blue eyes hungered like waiting vultures.

"Get a rope on him, Ivan Ivanovitch," he bellowed. "We'll teach this Muslim to drink vodka like a proper Christian before we cut his balls off!"

A rope fell in a tangled skein on Vaylance's legs.

"Hold off, Stepan. Don't mess him up too much," said Ivanovitch from his horse. "Maybe he's from one of the peaceful tribes. He has the look of the steppe about him. Not like those mountain devils we're after. . . . What's your tribe, boy?" Ivan Ivanovitch looked older than Stepan. On the lean side, he wore his black moustache curved like a Turkish scimitar.

"I'm Nogai," said Vaylance, trying to look as peaceable as he could. He wanted to conceal his Varkela origin from them, for the Cossacks had superstitions about the people who came out at night and drank human blood.

"You don't look like a Nogai," boomed Stepan, giving Vaylance another boot in the stomach. "Get up! Move! You're a prisoner of the Terek Cossacks, and if you're smart, you'll tell us where the rest of the Circassian infidels you came with are hiding."

"But I'm not Circassian," Vaylance insisted. "My people are from the steppe."

"You're too light-skinned for a Nogai," said Stepan, fingering the filigree hilt of his saber ominously.

"But he's dressed like one," said Ivan. "Leave him be. The ataman won't like it if you provoke an incident with one of the peaceful tribes."

"The ataman be damned! Him and that blasted doctor have turned you all into school boys and nursing sisters," said Stepan. "No soft-bellied book-learning for me. I'm for rendering this fellow's fat, here and now."

Vaylance's hope sprang up at the word "doctor." "It's the doctor that I've come to see," he cried. "You see, many members of my tribe are sick, and we thought that he might have the right medicine."

"That's a clever way to get a spy into the fort," said Stepan, his vulture's eyes yearning toward the long-awaited morsel. "We'll see how long you stick to that story." He bent down and grabbed the rope and began to loop it over Vaylance's arms.

Vaylance was not about to let himself be trussed like a hog for the butcher and lashed out with one foot, catching the Cossack in the knee. He swung at Stepan's head, but only managed to send the Cossack's fur-covered shapka flying. The struggle ended when Stepan threw his full weight on Vaylance and wrestled him to the ground. Vaylance howled his rage at being pinned helplessly, but stopped abruptly, when he felt the tips of his were-teeth begin to protrude from their little niches in his upper jaw. *If he sees that, I'm done for,* he thought and clamped his lips firmly shut. He might have used his teeth in self-defense. A well-placed bite could sever an artery. But he held back. His nature was to mend wounds, not make them, and better to be a live prisoner than to have his mutilated corpse displayed as a "Vampire."

Stepan flipped him onto his stomach and proceeded to knot the rope about his hands. If they took him to the fort, perhaps he could persuade someone there to let him speak to the doctor. But after the knot was tied, Stepan seemed to have other plans. He pulled a nine-inch dagger from the sheath in his waist band and began to toy with it. Vaylance watched the dagger, glinting in the last rays of the setting sun. He realized that they were not going to take him to the fort, at least not right away. . . .

"You know what we do with Tartar boys?" asked Stepan. "First we make a fire and heat up the knife nice and hot."

"Stepan Grigorovitch, I will not be party to this," said Ivan. "I wash my hands of you."

"If you go bearing tales about me," said Stepan to Ivan, "I will tell what I know about you and Pencherevsky's wife."

"If you do it will be the death of you, Stepan." Ivan rode away toward where the trees thickened in a snaky line between the hills.

The fire flamed up rapidly, fed with dung and resinous sage. Soot blackened the dagger except for the tip which glowed like a sunset.

I should have gone for the throat when I had a chance, thought Vaylance. Stepan knelt over him and stripped off one of Vaylance's felt boots. Vaylance felt the heat of the knife where Stepan held it inches from his bared sole. A good thing his father had taught him to trance, and with a certain mental exercise he willed his foot not to feel the pain. At one point, however, when trance failed him, his needle-like blood-teeth protruded full length like fangs of some venomous snake in its death agony.

"Gospodee! Thou art one of demonkind," cried Stepan.

He crossed himself and raised the knife, holding it poise over Vaylance's breast.

"Fire!" came a command.

A shot broke the air and Stepan fell full length over him. Vaylance looked up to see Ivan seated on horseback, his musket directed at Stepan. The sharp tang of black powder drifted on the air. With Ivan was a sturdy, gray-haired man with full red face as if he blew through some reeded instrument, his cheeks puffed out like the rebab player at a Tartar wedding.

"I came for . . . doctor," said Vaylance and lapsed into unconsciousness.

♦ ♦ ♦

When he awoke, Vaylance found himself in a large room with rows of cots. The windows were high up and small, allowing little daylight, which suited Vaylance's nocturnal eyes very well. He noted that his foot pained him terribly and was swathed in white bandages. Trance was only partially successful, as he was not yet totally adept at the art. In the dimness he could see men lying on cots about him. Some were bandaged, but many moaned and tossed in the grip of fever.

"So, you're awake, lad," a voice called to him from across the room. Vaylance saw what he had not noticed before—a desk stood in one corner with a battered old samovar steaming on one end. The large, red-faced man at the desk hailed him.

"Doctor Rimsky at your service. You must answer a few questions to satisfy my commanding officer. First of all, what are you doing here and what tribe are you?"

"I am Nogai," said Vaylance, "and I've come to find a cure for the black-water fever. Many of our tribe are dying of it and we have no medicine." Vaylance felt uncomfortable lying to this man. He felt a strange desire to trust this outblood doctor, but he feared the consequences.

"Well, I think we can do something about that," said Rimsky.

He picked up a parcel, wrapped in white paper and strolled over to the cot where Vaylance was lying.

"Cinchona bark from the new world," he said, peeling off the paper to reveal some brown, woody stuff. "It's a specific for malaria."

Vaylance touched the crumbly bark—an herbal remedy from the new world?

"Does it work?" he asked.

"Very well indeed," said Rimsky. "You see Plotinsky over there?"

Vaylance looked. A blond Russian soldier nodded to him from a bed across the room.

"Three days ago he was in the throes of fever, but you couldn't tell that from looking at him now."

Vaylance agreed. The blond soldier was bright-eyed—nothing of sickness about him.

"Will you sell me some of this bark, then?" Vaylance asked hopefully.

"No, because I would have to be there to administer the proper dosage. What we'll do is, I'll ride out with you as soon as you're well enough to travel, and we'll put an end to the epidemic among your people."

Vaylance's bubble of hope burst—having this outblood doctor cure the Nogai would not earn blood for Rayorka. Somehow he would have to convince this doctor to let him take the medicine to the Nogais himself.

"That would be much trouble for you," Vaylance ventured. "Couldn't you teach me the proper dosage? In my family we are shamans and healers, and I have often dosed illness with herbal preparations. If you tell me the strength of dose and when to administer it, it would save you much trouble."

"I'm not sure I would feel right entrusting the care of malarial patients to a shamanist. With all respect to your family, Vaylance, shamanism may be helpful in the sense that it deals with the soul and religious aspects of healing, but it cannot be a substitute for modern medicine."

It angered Vaylance to have his people's knowledge belittled in this way. He had seen his father cure illnesses that "modern medicine" could not. He'd even done a few of the more difficult soul-mendings himself. Somehow he must earn this doctor's trust and respect.

"Would it be all right if I went with you on your rounds? I'm sure I could learn a lot," he said.

"Now that's the sort of attitude I like," said Rimsky. "Love of learning. Do you read, boy? I'll set you to study a little surgery, until your foot heals up. Can't have you walking around on blistered feet."

"I can't read yet," said Vaylance, "but I'd like to learn." His mother had taught him the Russian alphabet. "There are whole other worlds in books," she used to say.

"Excellent," said Rimsky. "I'll send one of my Cossack students to read for you. You'll pick up a little knowledge and it will be good practice for him. That reminds me— you say your family are shamanists—have you ever heard of a tribe called Varkela? Supposedly they practice medicine in exchange for human blood."

Vaylance's blood turned to ice in his veins. Should he blurt it all out? Make his secret known?

"I've never heard of them," he said, hoping Rimsky would divulge a bit more.

"Probably nothing more than another Vampire legend," said Rimsky. "Still it is an intriguing proposition, is it not?"

"Yes, very," said Vaylance. "It would be proof that the drinking of blood is not in all cases evil." He thought the doctor looked at him a bit strangely.

◆ ◆ ◆

That afternoon, the young Cossack, Plotinsky, sat at the foot of Vaylance's bed and read to him from a text of anatomy. Vaylance was not surprised that Russian medicine seemed to know little of yin and yang, acupuncture, and the flow of Ki energy in touch healing, but there were also many things to learn from them, details of anatomy that could only have been learned by dissection of cadavers—a practice forbidden by the burial rites of most of the peoples of the steppe. He was fascinated with the fine detail in the pictures. "Whole other worlds in books," as his mother had often told him. The surgery text was even more wonderful and strange, with names of instruments of which he'd never heard: surgical forceps, amputating saws. He longed to be able to read the text himself and pestered Plotinsky to help him sound out the words.

That afternoon, when he felt well enough to hobble around with a crutch, he followed Rimsky on his rounds, and carefully observed his treatment of the *Great Fever*.

"It's important that malarial fever be caught early, before it progresses to the black-water stage," said Rimsky, "for then even cinchona bark will have little effect—and may even cause an adverse reaction."

"Now, then, Vaylance," he continued, "just to be sure we are working with the same disease, would you describe the symptoms of this 'black-water fever' your people suffer from?"

Vaylance wished he could say that his people didn't suffer from it at all, that it was an outblood disease, but he felt he'd better be consistent in his story. Dutifully he began to describe the symptoms he had observed among the Nogai Tartars.

"First come chills for several minutes to an hour. Next is fever that lasts four to six hours. Next is sweating and finally sleep. The patient awakens feeling much better, but in two to three days it comes again. After the second cycle, some may develop black urine and die. Others may have milder attacks which keep recurring at two to three day intervals. These do not die or develop black urine, but they may have the disease intermittently throughout life. And one must not take blood from them."

"You have very good clinical observation, Vaylance, to catch on to different forms of malaria, but your last statement about the blood—what does that mean?"

Vaylance mentally damned himself for letting that slip out. What he had meant was that his people did not take blood in payment from malarial patients, but rather from their relatives, for it had been found long ago that it was possible to transfer the disease to the next human one bit for payment, although the Varkela themselves were immune. He puzzled how to answer the question.

"Just an old custom of my people," he finally said.

Fortunately, Rimsky let the subject drop.

"I had a son who died," he mused. "He would have been just about your age." His eyes stared into the distance, as if reliving old pain.

How sad, thought Vaylance, who felt as if he had blundered into some sacred woodland shrine.

◆ ◆ ◆

During the course of the afternoon, Vaylance found that the treatment he sought consisted of giving a purgative, followed by hourly doses of a strong infusion of cinchona bark, given before the next attack was expected. It was apparently an effective treatment, for although some patients had recurrent bouts of fever, few reached the fatal black-water stage.

Late that afternoon Rimsky ushered Vaylance into his book-lined study and allowed him to peer through a small metal tube with glass lenses in it. The microcosm of "cavorting, wee beasties in a drop of water" fascinated him. Whole other worlds in a drop of pond water.

"There's a French doctor I correspond with, who believes that disease may be caused by infestations of this kind of tiny animals," said Rimsky.

On another slide, Rimsky pricked his finger and allowed a drop of blood to fall. Vaylance's mouth watered and his hunger pained him so that his blood-teeth began to protrude. But Rimsky, involved in putting a cover slide on the drop, did not notice. The blood on the slide was a viscous fluid filled with million of tiny, red, flattened discs. The delicious scent of fresh blood filled Vaylance's eager nostrils, and a sweet dizziness overtook him.

"Easy there, lad," the doctor caught him. "You seem a bit tipsy. Perhaps I was mistaken to let you up so soon. Go back and bed down again. I'll see you in the morning."

Vaylance was only too happy to have a bit of daytime sleep. His nocturnal pattern had been upset and blood-need ached hollowly through his vessels. Passing for an outblood Tartar was taking its toll. Another day had passed and he was still no closer to the cure that would feed his sister. He dreamed of Rayorka on her pallet, lifeless. He touched her and her body crackled, broke and blew away, like the dry leaves of autumn.

He awoke to find the doctor sitting on his bed talking to Plotinsky.

"Ah, there. He's awake," said Rimsky. "Bring the dose."

Plotinsky offered a beaker of the cinchona infusion.

"Just a preventative, Vaylance. This will keep you from contracting malaria yourself."

Vaylance was about to object that this wasn't necessary for him, but remembered that he had better go along with it to keep his story straight.

When he tasted the vile stuff, he wished he hadn't.

Bitter! His thin, pink dog-like tongue snaked out unbidden to wash the beastly stuff from his lips.

"Amazing," said Rimsky. "Do that again."

"What?" asked Vaylance, wishing he could bite off the foolish licking tongue that had betrayed him.

"Show me your tongue. There's something strange about it."

Vaylance complied, allowing his tongue to loll like a dog's. His mind raced to explain the anomaly.

"We in my family all have this deformity. It's an inherited trait," he said, feeling this was not quite the same as a lie.

"Very peculiar," said Rimsky, knotting bushy gray eyebrows over his nose. "Such a trait is differentiating to such an extent that I would venture that your family is a subspecies of *Homo sapiens*. *Homo sapiens lupus*, I would offer as a name. He looks a bit wolvish, don't you think, Plotinsky? Perhaps we've stumbled on a new race—must write this up and send it to a scientific journal. Drink the rest, lad. We don't want you getting sick on us."

Vaylance finished the vile liquid, avoiding the little bits of bark in the residue. Oh, what he would have given for a dose of fresh human blood in a similar proportion. But one could not ask for blood unless one had earned through healing, and one certainly could not expect to get it here. The Russians and Cossacks played by different rules than the nomadic Tartars. Perhaps he would have to stoop to blood-theft in the night to feed his need. His teeth yearned for the thick red juice of life. It was painful to lie here in bed thinking about blood. How much more so Rayorka! He resolved to put his own selfish thirst aside until he'd solved the problem: how to gain the cure for malaria so that the Nogai would come to pay them once again. Somehow he must convince Rimsky of his ability to prepare the dosage on his own.

"If I may, will you let me prepare the dosages today?" he asked, thinking that perhaps Rimsky would perceive that he was capable and yield the bark to him.

"I'm afraid your mathematics are a bit naive, Vaylance, and I would have to spend many hours to teach you what I can do in a few minutes for myself," said Rimsky.

It was true. Vaylance's knowledge of the Russian system of weights and measures was sadly lacking. He'd forgotten much since he'd lived with his mother. His people had their own way of measuring dosages, based on body weight, age, and severity of symptoms, but this would not help him until he was able to translate from Dr. Rimsky's system to his own.

"But let me at least help you," he insisted. Perhaps if he learned enough, through watching, he could take the precious bark and reproduce the cure himself. But that would be stealing, like the blood-thief who comes in the night, leaving nothing in return.

◆ ◆ ◆

It was a long day, measuring dosages for each patient. Every time Vaylance thought he had gotten it right, Rimsky would point out that he had forgotten to carry a figure to the tens column or had failed to convert from grams to drachmas. He was about to despair of ever learning the system when another plan suggested itself.

Rimsky was cleaning up his work bench and offering Vaylance to share a glass of tea from the samovar when Plotinsky came in, concern showing in his plump, healthy face, and said, "They've brought her again. She's mad as a rabid dog this time."

Vaylance noted that Rimsky's red-faced jovial visage became a few shades paler. He shook his head sadly and said, "There's little I can do but restrain her and give her a sleeping draught. But tell the parents to wait and I'll come."

Insanity—a disease of the soul—this was something he understood; perhaps if he offered his services, he could win Rimsky's confidence and achieve his goal.

"My people know how to cure madness, sir," he ventured. "Perhaps if you'd let me try. . . ." He hoped it was a simple form of madness. Spareen had been right. It had been mostly luck with the Cheremiss boy. If only his father were here. . . .

But Rimsky waved him aside. "There is no cure for madness, lad. It comes and goes as it wills. Would you have us rattle bones and chant, where modern methods fail? Get back to your bed. I'll be around to see you later."

Much disgruntled, Vaylance was led back to the infirmary and made to change into his night shirt. He pulled the voluminous garment over his clothes and disrobed under it to avoid showing Plotinsky his fury chest, belly, and loins. He pulled the sheets up and feigned rest until Plotinsky left, then crept from bed and made his way down the hallway.

He quickly covered the distance to the study and stood just beyond the doorway, watching the scene in the next room. A young girl, her hands tied behind her back, crouched on the floor, making low animal noises in her throat. Dr. Rimsky tried to raise her and place her in a chair, but she screamed and fought him. Her fear-crazed eyes rolled wildly and she continued to scream through clenched teeth. A drool of spittle rolled down her chin. A plump woman, probably the girl's mother, covered her eyes and wept. The father put an arm around his wife and said to Rimsky, "You see how it is? We just can't control her. She persists in these wild rages."

The girl, mewling like some wounded mountain panther, kicked over the chair and it clattered to the floor. Her father reached her in two strides, took her by the shoulders and began to shake her.

"Stop it!" he cried. "By all that's holy, stop it!"

"Wait!" called Vaylance from his post by the door. "That's not the way at all!"

A hush fell on the room, as everyone stared in his direction. Even the mad girl ceased to scream and looked his way. Vaylance fixed his eyes on her and began to speak to her, as one speaks to comfort a frightened horse. Doctor Rimsky made as if to object, but Vaylance waved him silent, never taking his eyes from the terrified orbs of the girl.

"I know what I'm doing, Doctor," he said. "Do not interfere."

He fervently hoped that this was a form of madness that would succumb to his methods and that he would prove himself worthy of the respect of this outblood doctor. Because the girl had stopped screaming, all seemed willing to watch, spellbound, as Vaylance, looking spectral in his nightshirt, crossed the room, arms outstretched, and placed his hands on the sick girl's head.

Kneeling down beside her, he began to sing the chant as he had heard his father do so many times. If I can just bring it off, he thought, I will open another world to you, my outblood doctor. Carefully, carefully he repeated the words and felt the spasms of Ki energy flowing through his finger—rush and flow, rush and flow like waves on a beach. The smooth flow of his Ki sought to overrule the jagged flux of her terrified mind. His eyes probed the depths of hers, seeking the source of her terror, and, then, like a rending tear, his mind's eye opened and viewed her soul as it struggled with a demon spirit. The snout of the fox-like face of the demon smiled back at him. A word tripped too swiftly across Vaylance's tongue, and in an instant the demon was off, leading Vaylance's soul on a merry chase through the many twistings and turnings of the maze of madness, its white plume of fox tail dipping and dodging. Vaylance gave up the chase as fruitless in a few moments, but it was already too late. His own soul was trapped in the never-ending tunnels of a tangled mind.

"I was a fool," he thought, "to think I could handle a madness like this with so little experience." The flat gray walls of the tunnel began to close in on him, and he felt panic rising in his soul, for he feared this time he was indeed lost to the eternal dream. In his fear he cried out, and suddenly there loomed up before him the bone-faced mask of the gray ghost stag with green fire playing through its antlers.

"Follow me," it said. "I will show you the source."

Vaylance followed the gaunt form obediently as it led deeper and deeper into the convoluted turnings of the crazed mind. Finally the corridor opened into a small room that must have been the center of the maze. There, at the middle, a huge stone crushed a small tree that attempted to reach around the boulder with branches grotesque and stunted. But the stone seemed to totally smother the young tree, repressing its natural upward growth, crushing the life out of it.

"Remove the stone," said the stag.

Vaylance placed his shoulder against the rock and pushed vigorously. On the third try, he dislodged it and the stone fell to the floor, breaking in many shards.

Already the young tree appeared more alive. New shoots began to reach upward and the crooked branches to straighten. It was still crooked in places, but a fine new trunk was rising where the stone had been. The gray ghost stag, trailing mist and grave-clothes, led him safely back through the maze, and he came to himself again where he knelt, staring into the lackluster eyes of the mad girl, his hands on her head. He sang to her in the old language and felt the flow of her brain smooth out. The former jagged flux became calm as a pond with gliding swans. Finally he broke contact with his fingers and she slumped against him. He was untying her bonds when she awoke as from a restful sleep.

"Mother, Father, what is happening?" she asked.

Immediately the girl's mother was on her knees, hugging the girl to her breast.

"You might give her something to eat. I imagine she's hungry," said Vaylance, and thought of his own hunger. His veins ached hollowly and he wondered how long before his empty heart would cease to function and he would die "the dry death." Faintness dragged him down.

He was suddenly aware of Rimsky, kneeling beside him, putting an arm around his shoulders. "Simply amazing," said the doctor. "I would never have believed if I hadn't seen for myself."

Rimsky helped him up and he leaned on the doctor's strong arm all the way back to his bed. Rimsky took a panel screen and drew it around the bed to insure privacy.

"Well, lad, I'm most indebted to you for what you did tonight. It seems there are things you can teach me and I was presumptuous to assume that your shamanism was a totally useless art."

"She is not totally healed yet," said Vaylance. "Now comes the talking cure where we must let her speak of her sorrows; then the rest is up to her whether she be healed or not."

"I'm so much in your debt," said Rimsky, "that I'm willing to pay the cost of such a healing." Saying this, he undid his cuff and rolled up his sleeve. "This is the accepted method of payment, is it not?" He offered his arm for Vaylance's inspection as any Tartar of steppe.

◆ ◆ ◆

Vaylance was filled with mistrust for a moment. Was Rimsky mocking his hunger, trying to lure him into betraying himself? He looked into the older man's eyes and saw fear. The arm fairly trembled. Rimsky was taking a great risk in trusting a suspected Vampire.

To soothe the fear, Vaylance began to intone softly the gentle rhythm of the "sleeping song," but he did not let Rimsky slip into so deep a trance that he was unaware of what was happening.

"We do it like this," he said before slipping one of his long, thin incisor teeth into the proper vein. The juice of life flowed into him in waves, and he counted with heartbeats until his proper fee had been extracted, then withdrew and healed the wound with a swipe of his pink dog-like tongue.

"But how did you know what I was?" he asked of Rimsky.

"I didn't at first," said Rimsky, "but I remembered what an old Kalmuck servant of mine told me of another race that traded blood for healing. When I saw your tongue and fur and the gaps in your upper jaw for retractable teeth, I knew there must be some truth in it. But the medical prowess I had dismissed as so many tall tales. One always takes stories of miracles with a grain of salt."

"But what of the others?" asked Vaylance, attempting to peer around the screen.

"They must not know of your true nature, lad. There are too many of them with more imagination than brains. A 'Vampire' among us could not be accepted. But your secret is safe with me, Vaylance. From what I've learned from my old servant, Subachi, your race is not evil, but really a very honest, fair-minded people, and your need for blood is much less than the mythical Vampire."

Vaylance was overcome with emotion and didn't know what to say. Where he'd expected only fear and hatred, if discovered, he'd found a friend, who accepted him as he was without misunderstanding.

He told Rimsky about Rayorka and her blood-need.

"Few women survive puberty," he said, "but she must live, and others like her, for the sake of our race, or we will die out within a few generations."

"In that case, I shall entrust the fever bark to you with proper instructions. But promise you'll come back from time to time. I'm sure we could learn a lot from each other. You've certainly opened my eyes to the shamanistic way of healing."

"When my sister is well, I will come back," said Vaylance. "And if I come, will you teach me to read and write? I would like to write down the healing ways of my people, so that a whole world of wisdom will not pass away, if we should die out."

That very day Vaylance set out with a parcel of cinchona bark in his saddlebags. He urged his horse to travel swiftly, for he knew he carried life to the Nogais and to his sister.

Pausing for a brief moment to look back on the fort, he wiped his running nose on his jacket sleeve. His allergies would always plague him, he knew, but a certain healing had taken place inside his own soul. With Rimsky a whole other world of friendship had opened to him, and he knew he would be back soon.

# SPAREEN AMONG
# THE COSSACKS

SPAREEN, THE VARKELA leechman, shifted his weight in the saddle as he paused to survey the Cossack fort at Groznoi. To the east, high walls made of perpendicular logs jutted skyward against the flat blue horizon of the steppe. To the south its irregular perimeter marked a huge gap in the distant white teeth of the Caucasus Mountains. The golden-eyes mare lowered her head to pick at small yellow flowers of toadflax among the tall grass, oblivious to his concern. He wondered why his brother, Vaylance, had so urgently summoned him here. For a healing? For help in dreamwalking? Or perhaps out of sheer loneliness for one of his own kind in his self-imposed exile here among the Cossacks.

Spareen's thin, hollow blood-teeth slipped involuntarily

out of their little niches in his upper jaw. He quickly retracted them again, like a cat's claws. It would never do to let the Cossacks see those, with their silly superstitions. People like Spareen, who came out at night and drank human blood, were viewed with suspicion among the Slavs, even though Varkela were only honest leechmen, collecting the proper fee for healing from a carefully placed bite on arm or leg.

He wondered how Vaylance fared here among the Russians and Cossacks, who might call a leechman Vampire if he were indiscreet in collecting the *blood-price*. Enough worrying about that, thought Spareen whose were-teeth ached hungrily in his jaw. Vaylance must be receiving some form of payment, or he wouldn't have survived here so long.

To the untrained eye, Spareen could have appeared a Tartar, but any Tartar would recognize him as Varkela by the way he tied his ink-black hair back in a tail, and by his white doe-skin shirt and trousers. He was a hulking big fellow with large hands and feet, handsome in a rustic sort of way, slightly oriental about the eyes, but with a nose straight as a plowshare.

He gave his mare a nudge with his calves to let her know that he'd finished his contemplations, but instead of proceeding to the fort, she reached around and tugged with her teeth at his faded doe-skin trousers and fixed him with those all-too-knowing golden eyes.

"Now don't make any trouble for yourself here," she admonished him in the horse language that only the Varkela understand.

"Make trouble? And how might I do that?" asked Spareen mildly.

"You know what I mean. So don't waste that innocent look on me. The last time we came in from the steppe, you got drunk, got into a fight, and almost lost the nomad yurt you sleep in over some silly wager. Your temper will be the ruination of both of us," said the mare.

"I suppose you're right," sighed Spareen. "Ever since that she-witch Varkura dumped me, I've been out of sorts."

"You shouldn't be so hot-headed, Spareen. Learn to talk your way out of a fight. Last month you were so banged-up, you needed more doctoring than most of your patients."

"Not half as banged-up as that fellow was when I threw him through the pot-house wall," Spareen smirked, remembering. "But you're right. If some Cossack did punch me out and happened to take a look in my mouth, then I'd really be in trouble. So for your sake and mine, I shall keep a tight rein on my temper. Does that satisfy you?"

"Only if you mean it," said the mare, but she let go of his pant leg and set off for the fort gate at a jog-trot. The evening sun reddened on the horizon like a bullet wound. A plover took wing in front of them, keening plaintively, and settled in a hummock of sage further on.

"You're a fine one to advise me," said Spareen. "Didn't I raise you from a foal and suckle you on a sponge?" But he knew it was wasted breath, for if she deigned to answer at all, she would only say that horses age faster than men and are therefore wiser.

They passed unchallenged at the sentry box and entered the stanitza, passing Cossack houses raised up on stilts to avoid the spring flooding of the river Terek. This late in summer they resembled boat docks at low water and were connected by footbridge galleries that ran above the hard-packed dirt streets.

Of the many buildings, one was a large one-story with windows placed high up. Surely this was the infirmary his brother had described. Spareen dismounted, unhooked his saddlebags and checked the tools of his trade:

a pharmacopoeia of herbs, two needles, two little scalpels of German steel, and a small tin biscuit box holding a bit of moldy bread dough. Slinging the bags over his shoulder, he bounded up the steps, two at a time, and knocked at the door.

A robust, red-faced Russian with graying hair and eyebrows answered the knock, and Spareen asked for his brother in the best of his Tartar-accented Russian. "Spareen!" a voice cried from within the depths of the house, and a thin, scholarly young man with pince-nez perched on his plowshare nose pushed past the Russian, flung himself on Spareen and kissed him. Vaylance was half a head shorter than Spareen, built on a more delicate scale, with small, deft hands, skilled to bind up wounds with small, neat stitches. He wore his dark, ragged locks trimmed to the collar after the manner of the Russian soldiers, and one would have hardly thought that he and Spareen were brothers, except for that nose and those dark eyes that glowed with a certain mysterious inner light of their own.

When Vaylance hugged him, Spareen could not resist the temptation to poke his elder brother in the ribs. Ticklish as ever, Vaylance flinched and swatted Spareen's shovel-sized paw away.

"Do I take it that you two know each other?" asked the ruddy-faced Russian with an amused grin.

"Forgive me," said Vaylance. "This is my brother, Spareen—I told you he'd come—and this," he said indicating the Russian, "is Dr. Vladimer Ivanovitch Rimsky, my instructor in the science of medicine."

"He's being modest," said the sanguine Rimsky, putting an arm around Vaylance's thin shoulders. "I learn more from Vaylance about the Varkela art of healing then he does from me about the 'science of medicine.' He works more cures than I do around this place. I don't know what I'd do without him."

He turned to Vaylance. "Get your brother settled in your quarters and you can explain to him our problem."

Spareen followed Vaylance back into the depths of the house, past a room full of occupied cots, the infirmary, and past a small room leaking sharp chemical and mild herbal odors, the pharmacy. Vaylance's room was small and dark, a comfort to nocturnal Varkela eyes. A single candle burned in a niche before an icon showing the Madonna and Child surrounded by wild animals in varying poses of adoration, Grushnitsky's "Virgin of the Beasts."

"I dreamed your soul-beast yesterday," said Spareen, recalling the regal stag poised as if for flight near the edge where the steppe meets woodland. "Was it a sending?"

"It was," said Vaylance. "I sent for you because I need your help in a healing. The Russian colonel Barikoff lies ill with putrescent ulcers on his leg that won't heal, and yesterday he became feverish. I've tried all my knowledge of herbal febrifuges, even the Peruvian fever bark, to no avail. Healer's touch brings him some relief from pain, and moments of consciousness, but it soon passes and I fear for his life."

"Then I suppose you will be wanting to try the mold-cure," said Spareen, thinking grimly of the last time he'd been called upon to perform this type of healing.

"Precisely," said Vaylance. "Do you have the mold starter with you?"

"I do," said Spareen. "I always come prepared for the worst." He took out the precious tin box containing the mold that his family had nurtured and nursed for generations, a special, potent strain, rapid-growing if given a special food and dormant for months if stored correctly.

"I suppose I must begin then," sighed Spareen, prying off the lid. He heated his scalpel in the candle flame, allowed it to cool, and carefully extracted a portion of the bread dough. This he placed in his mouth and began to chew and mix with saliva until he had a soupy mess, then he sucked the mixture up into his hollow blood-teeth. He could feel the stuff settle in the reservoir of his naso-dental sinuses where the blood that he normally ingested would be strained for antibodies before entering his blood stream. Spareen's reluctance to do the mold-cure was based on the fact that pressure from the mold's growth caused terrible sinus headaches. But the process produced a precious healing liquor which could be injected into the patient via the retractable Varkelan blood-teeth.

"When you start to feel a headache coming on," said Vaylance, "take a little wine into your stomach. I'll put my hands on your face and draw out the pain."

A good idea, thought Spareen, who somewhat envied Vaylance's gift of healer's touch. Pity I was the only one in the family with stout enough constitution to withstand the ravages of the mold-cure, he mused. The worst part of it was that while the damn stuff was lodged in his sinuses, he couldn't take blood. It had been a week since his last payment from the Nogai tartars, and he ached for the thick red juice of life. This thinking led him to a question.

"Vaylance, how do they pay you here? Surely the Russians and Cossacks don't pay you the *blood-price* as the Tartars do."

"No," said Vaylance. "I have to resort to a mild form of subterfuge. After the patient is well enough, I invite him back for a quiet cup of tea and one last 'examination,' and if he should happen to fall asleep and awaken with an insect bite in the nook of the arm, he is not much alarmed. It makes me feel somewhat dishonest, but Rimsky won't have it any other way. He fears the superstitious would misunderstand and take me for a Vampire—which reminds me, Spareen—while you are here, do not do anything that might draw undo attention to yourself, or reveal your peculiar nature. My position here depends on it. I can't afford to be found out."

"I understand," said Spareen and mustered up his good intentions. Outbloods were so gullible, it was easy to take advantage of them, especially in matters concerning wagers on houses, but he would restrain himself. Considering the headache he would have, he would probably not feel up to any foolery.

"You must also understand," said Vaylance, "that this cure may be crucial to my staying here. You see, for the past year, Rimsky has provided for my support, and an army surgeon doesn't make that much. My hope is that if we heal this Barikoff, he can provide a bit of money for my upkeep here so that I can continue to study outblood medicine with Rimsky and teach him the ways of our people."

"We will have to wait and see," said Spareen. "The mold-cure doesn't always work, you know."

"I know," said Vaylance. "You lost one of your Tartars last time, didn't you?"

"True. Soodshi-Noyon, the Kalmuck chieftain died under my hands of the same thing you describe—except the pus from his wound was foul green and strange-smelling. How does the colonel's wound look?"

"Yellow drainage. The usual pus odor."

"It sounds hopeful then. I'd better make a solution of water and corn flower and suck it up to feed the mold. It usually takes a day and a half before I'm ready. Let's go have a look at the patient."

The two brothers took the footbridge that passed over the wheel-rutted, hard-packed street, crossing to the officers' quarters. Rimsky was already present when Spareen followed his brother into the bare-beamed sickroom. He noted that a large earthen stove filled one corner of the room, and nestled in a niche of the chimney a samovar hissed cheerfully. But the room was dominated by a huge Russian krovat, a high, narrow couch-like bed, richly carved and cushioned, where a waxy-skinned, unshaven older man lay propped up with one leg slung over the side to rest on a footstool. The inhabitant of the bed did not appear to be conscious, and Rimsky was squatting on the floor, his paunch protruding like a bullfrog's, dabbing with a napkin at the angry raw flesh bordering the ulcer. A buttery pustulence oozed from the center, drying into crusts, and the red outline of an inflamed vein could be seen leading away from the excrescence toward the heart—a very bad sign indeed. But the most unsettling aspect for Spareen was a slight greenish discoloration in the crusts at the edge of one of the ulcers. He pointed this out to Vaylance saying:

"The ulcer on the leg of Soodshi-Noyon began to green in a similar manner."

"Strange," said Vaylance. "I didn't notice it yesterday."

"When will this mold-cure of yours be ready?" asked Rimsky, standing up and discarding the discolored rag in a basin.

"Spareen says a day and a half," said Vaylance. "I'm afraid all we can do is wait until then. I hope he can hold on that long."

The remainder of that evening, Spareen spent following Rimsky and Vaylance on their rounds. The Russian methods of healing were not that much different in many respects from the usual Varkela treatment. A major difference was that the Russian doctor had many metal tools for a variety of surgeries. Spareen cast covetous eyes on the bone cutter. With such a tool, he could amputate unsalvageable limbs with much less trauma. What he wouldn't have given for one of those when he had served as medic to a Circassian tribe in one of their innumerable wars against the Cossacks back in '39.

And this fellow Rimsky wasn't the usual condescending

European-trained doctor. He seemed to have a lot of respect for the Varkela way of healing, even to the extent of having Vaylance teach him about the flow of *ki* energy in touch healing and the controlling of pain with Chinese needles.

Vaylance stopped to joke with one of the patients, his small, deft fingers kneading the pressure points along the spine. It was good to see Vaylance happy again after that long bout with melancholia. There were those of his people who thought him a bit addled—it was Favarka, her death that did it, they said—for here he was healing among the Cossacks, taking instruction from a Russian doctor rather than from an esteemed shaman of the steppe and, worse, accepting the religion of the cross-worshippers, anathema to the Varkela. But Spareen knew his brother wasn't crazy, and apparently life at the fort agreed with him, for his color was good, not like one who suffers from blood-need.

Rimsky retired at midnight, leaving the two brothers to talk until dawn. When the sun showed in the east, they drew hot water for tea from Rimsky's battered old bot-bellied samovar and retired to Vaylance's darkened room to take their daytime sleep.

Vaylance arose at 4:00 in the afternoon, an indecent hour to Spareen, whose head was beginning to feel heavy and hot from the mold-cure. He could hear his brother moving about the room. He cringed at the scrape of a chair and ground his teeth at the small clicking and tinkling noises of something being stirred in a glass bottle. Damned inconsiderate of Vaylance to be up so early, banging around.

Rimsky appeared in the doorway. "Is the laudanum ready?" he asked. "Our amputee, Orloff, is in much pain."

"It's ready," said Vaylance. "Would you like me to go

and sit up with the colonel tonight? You must be awfully tired."

"No," said Rimsky, "because tonight Dimitry has invited you to a party at Ustenka's, and I insist that you attend."

"A party? Me? That's thoughtful of him," said Vaylance.

"You're not going to leave me here to suffer while you go to a party, are you?" moaned Spareen after Rimsky left the room.

"Of course not. You're coming with me."

Spareen moaned even louder at that.

"Come on," said Vaylance, laying a cool hand on the bridge of Spareen's nose. "I have to go. This is a first for me. The Russian soldiers and the Cossacks don't usually invite me to their social gatherings. Perhaps they've finally decided to accept me in spite of my Tartar taint."

Beginning to feel a bit better, Spareen sat up. Vaylance's cool fingers seemed to suck out the pain like small mouths.

"You worry about what a bunch of Cossacks think of you?"

"Not that so much," said Vaylance, "but it has been lonely here. This Dimitry—I cured his horse of lameness—he's the first friend I've made here, except for Rimsky."

At 7:00 p.m. Dimitry, a burly, blond Russian with clean-shaven boyish cheeks, arrived, and Vaylance asked if Spareen might also come to the party.

"I'll dress him like a proper Russian," Vaylance promised. "That way people won't accuse you of being too friendly with the Tartars."

"I'm sure Ustenka won't mind," said Dimitry. "She was asking earlier who that handsome Tartar was, who rode in this evening. Just tell your brother not to run off with my Ustenka. I hope to run off with her myself this evening."

A thought tickled at the edge of Spareen's mind. If there were women at this party who could be witched, perhaps he'd have a bit of fun. And if there were one among them who was wolf-minded—that is, if she would not come when he witched her with his dark Varkela eyes—then she was an equal, and he might pursue that one even more. He felt a vague stirring in the roots of his belly fur and pulled himself up short in his thinking. He was, after all, here to help Vaylance in a healing and he'd promised—no foolishness.

He followed Vaylance back to his room to dress.

"Here, wear these trousers of mine." Vaylance offered him tight-fitting Russian pants. "I'll see if Rimsky can spare you a shirt. You're too big in the shoulders to fit anything of mine."

Vaylance left the room. A few minutes later he returned, bearing a white cotton shirt with a ruffle down the front.

"Will there be women at this party?" asked Spareen.

"Of course," said Vaylance. "But don't get your hopes up. As long as I've been here, I've yet to meet one woman who's wolf-minded. But, tell me, how is your relationship with that Tartar lady coming?"

"Like this and like that," said Spareen. "She's not the least bit wolvish, but if we could get a child, I'd marry her. So far I've wasted enough of my seed on her to raise up an army. And you know how father is. When he found out I was seeing an outblood, I thought he was going to cut off my cock and ship me to Constantinople in leg irons."

"Father's a smart old wolf. He knows where you go when you sneak off during the daytime. . . ."

"How come you never got caught?" asked Spareen.

"Oh, but I did," said Vaylance. "My career was not quite as illustrious as yours, Spareen. I only got laid twice before I got married, and both times father gave me the lecture about not wasting our seed on the outblood whores with whom we cannot get children."

"He's a hypocrite. Our own sister is a half-blood out of a Cossack woman."

"A wolf-minded Cossack woman, don't forget." Vaylance fussed with the collar at Spareen's throat.

"But that's the whole point," said Spareen. "What do they expect us to do with so few wolf-minded women around?"

"You might ask father to arrange a courtship for you. Surely there must be a woman of the blood looking for an extra husband. What about Varkura over in the Nogai territory?"

Spareen's throat constricted at the unhappy memory. "We tried her already. She turned me down. Valkeen said she'd take me in three years. But what do I do in the meantime?"

"My poor brother. How you suffer!" said Vaylance in mock sympathy.

"That's fine for you to say. You got married off at 17 and to someone wolf-minded too." Spareen realized he shouldn't have mentioned this, for he saw the old sadness come into Vaylance's eyes, but the sadness slipped away as quickly as it had come, and Vaylance said:

"All I can tell you is that some day a Varkela woman, or perhaps a wolf-minded outblood, will ride through your territory, and your heart will mount up and ride after her into the fullness of joy. That's all I can say. Now button down those cuffs—there you are. Let's go."

When they went out to meet Dimitry, Vaylance stopped to confer a moment with Rimsky. "Send for me and I will come if anyone is in much pain. I have my Chinese needles with me in my pocket." He patted his waistcoat where a small bulge protruded.

They descended the steps to the boardwalk and made their way between houses down into the street. The

Milky Way spread across the sky like a dusting of corn flour on black bread. On the wind came the aroma of flowers neatly planted in boxes in front of some of the houses, and occasionally the odor of a chicken coop.

"What's this mysterious illness that keeps you from going out in the daytime?" Dimitry asked of Vaylance.

Spareen almost laughed out loud, but caught his brother's warning glance and smothered the impulse.

"I don't know the name of it," said Vaylance. "Something long and scientific. Dr. Rimsky knows it. It makes my eyes very sensitive to light, so that I prefer to sleep days."

"Yet you seem quite well most of the time."

"Fortunately," said Vaylance, "it's not a severe case. My brother has the same affliction."

Clever of Vaylance, thought Spareen, to explain his nocturnal habits in such a manner.

When they reached the house where Ustenka and her mother lived, the party was already in progress. An attractive young Cossack woman with auburn hair greeted them at the door.

"Ustenka, may I present our surgeon's assistant, Vaylance, and brother Spareen," said Dimitry.

Ustenka nodded and raised her eyes to meet Spareen's. The eyes of a sheep, he thought and although she was pretty, his finely tuned Varkela nose brought him the flat smell of an outblood woman, nothing of interest here.

She invited them in and was introducing them around when Spareen noticed a red-bearded Cossack eyeing them with contempt.

"Who's that?" he asked his brother.

"Ivan Stepanovitch," said Vaylance. "He's a rude lout, always looking for a fight. Don't let anything he says provoke you, Spareen. I know how to handle him."

They sat down at the table across from Ivan, for there

was no other place to sit. Ustenka brought them cups of Chikkur, the local red wine, and a large bowl of strawberries and clotted cream. Spareen declined the strawberries, but downed a cup of the wine.

"So, your brother is a drinker," cried Dimitry, slapping Spareen on the back. "Another round over here, Ustenka."

The red-bearded Cossack studied them thoughtfully, stroking his bandoliers on the front of his coat, and then turned to one of his fellows and said quite loudly, so that Vaylance and his friends might overhear, "Is it true that our esteemed surgeon's assistant is really a smelly goat-doctor from the steppe?"

There was a painful lull in the conversation. Spareen's anger impelled him to reach down and pull a knife from his boot, but before he could bring it above table level, he felt Vaylance's small hand grip his wrist like a manacle. He saw that Vaylance's other hand restrained Dimitry's balled fist.

"Quite true," Vaylance addressed the onlookers. "I practiced on the smelly goats, that I might learn better how to care for Cossack soldiers."

Everyone laughed good-naturedly at this and the uncomfortable tension passed. Vaylance whispered, "You two young hot heads could have provoked a duel. Show a little more sense."

But red-bearded Ivan seemed determined to needle the newcomers. He produced a balalaika, strummed a few chords and said:

"I have studied the Tartars for many years, and I've found that they are a genteel folk, as will be evidenced by this Tartar song that I'm about to sing for you." And he began to sing Russian words to a tune that he must have devised himself, for it was no Tartar song:

> *"I'm a Tartar, a mean and evil Tartar,*
> *And I leave a trail of red behind.*
> *I take delight in stirring up a fight,*
> *And roasting little babies on a bun*
> *'Til they're done.*
>
> *"I'm a Tartar, a mean and nasty Tartar.*
> *I smell like uncle Ivan's dirty socks.*
> *I drink kumiss and the water that I piss.*
> *When I want a wench I beat her in the head*
> *'Til she's dead."*

Spareen felt insulted by this but, inhibited by Vaylance's presence, decided to retaliate in song rather than fisticuffs. He reached across the table, borrowed the instrument from Ivan and said:

"I've studied the Cossacks for many years, and I've observed that they are such a cultured folk that no one can outdo them at gentility." He strummed a tune on the balalaika and raised his mighty baritone in song:

> *"I'm a Cossack and I stink*
> *From the vodka that I drink*
> *And the urine that I use*
> *For my obligations.*
>
> *"I'm a lazy lout.*
> *People know, without a doubt,*
> *Screwing donkeys is*
> *My only occupation."*

Ivan Stepanovitch's hand strayed to the rapier that hung at his side. "Say that again, Tartar," he snarled.

"Wait, wait . . . you misunderstood my brother," Vaylance interposed. "You see, he used a Tartar word in that song. The Tartar meaning of 'screw' is 'to brush.' So, you see, what Spareen meant to say was, 'brushing donkeys is my only occupation.' "

"There's no such word in Tartar," muttered Spareen, under his breath.

"You'd better pretend there is," Vaylance whispered back. "Remember, Spareen, I will be held accountable for your behavior."

Ivan Stepanovitch threw back his head and laughed, his teeth marking a white line between his fiery beard and mustache.

"I'll forgive you this time," he said, "if you'll promise not to foul our fair mother-tongue with Tartar words that sound like profanities."

At that moment a soldier came into the house and looked around the room until he spied the table where Vaylance was sitting. He pushed his way through the crowded tables, and said:

"The doctor needs your assistance."

Vaylance stood and excused himself. Before leaving, he warned Spareen, "Remember our agreement. No foolishness."

After he left, Dimitry turned to Spareen and said: "Tell me a bit about your people. Vaylance tells me that you're not really Tartars, like the Kalmucks and Nogais."

"That's right," said Spareen. "We were here before the Mongols came. According to our tradition, we rode with Attila the Hun. Some of us settled in Hungary and The Balkans, but most of us stayed in Caucasia or on the steppe."

"You're descended from the Huns, then?" asked Dimitry. "The people who drank the blood of their enemies?"

"No, we are not Huns either. The Huns were probably accused of drinking blood because we rode with them. We are a separate race entirely. According to our tradition, we originally came from the Altai Mountain area, north of Mongolia."

"What did you mean about drinking blood? Did your people actually do that?"

Spareen was feeling a bit uncomfortable and wasn't sure how to answer this. Finally he said, "A long time ago, we were a race of physicians, and it was our custom to take, in payment for healing, small amounts of human blood. But it's just an old story."

"I should hope so!" said Dimitry.

Across the table Ivan began to pick out a lively dance tune on his instrument. "Let's get this party going!" he cried.

Soon people were on their feet, pushing back the tables. A line of dancers formed, weaving in and out around each other in a difficult pattern. Dimitry got up to dance. Spareen accepted another cup of wine and sat back in his chair, putting his feet up on another. He was beginning to feel the effects of the wine. It seemed to help the heaviness in his head; however too much would have the opposite effect, and he realized he'd better stop soon. But not just yet.

Dimitry came stomping back to the table and sat down, his blond bulk looking totally dejected. He kicked at one of the table legs.

"What's wrong, my friend?" asked Spareen.

"That stuck-up girl, Ustenka, won't dance with me, since an officer has taken an interest in her tail."

Spareen looked across the room to where the pretty Cossack girl flirted with one of the Russian officers.

"I can get her to come over here," he offered.

"I doubt it." said Dimitry. "But go ahead and try, if you think you can." He apparently expected Spareen to make some excuse to go up and speak to the girl. But Spareen just leaned back in his chair and half closed his eyes, carefully following her movements.

Ustenka looked up suddenly with a questioning glance, but then went back to talking to her officer. The officer caught her around the waist and pulled her down on his lap, but she jumped up from the table, blushing and giggling. She turned back to the table where the Russian officers sat laughing, and hesitated, looking again at Spareen. He nodded to her, indicating that she should come join his table. Slowly, with a puzzled stare, she approached.

"What's the matter, Ustenka?" one of the men at the officers' table called after her. She ignored him and came up beside Spareen.

"May I join your table?" she asked.

Dimitry moved closer to Spareen and made room for her to pull up a chair.

"How did you do that?" he asked Spareen.

Spareen was feeling reckless. The wine was beginning to go to his head. It felt good after that awful headache, but he would have to stop soon. Just one more cup.

"I can get any woman in this room," he drawled, "if she'll look me in the eye just once."

"What rubbish!" exclaimed Ivan, his teeth flashing under a flaming mustache. "If you Tartar infidels are so handy with women, bring us a few more."

"All right, I will," declared Spareen. He waved to a dark-haired girl and caught her eye. She came and joined their table.

"Nothing to it," he said.

A stocky girl carrying a plate of cakes was the next to meet Spareen's entrapping gaze. She too came over and sat down. The Russian enlisted men at the table were making the most of their chance to engage the Cossack girls in conversation. Ivan, however, was so fascinated by Spareen's way with women that he all but ignored the pretty girl sitting next to him.

"Try that one," he would say, indicating another woman with a reputation for being unapproachable. Some of them took longer than others, but eventually each of them, after a few moments of his attention, would look around to see who was staring at her and meet his beckoning eyes. After a while many of the young men came over and joined Spareen's table, since that was where most of the women were.

Ivan had an idea and moved around the table to be closer to Spareen. He pressed his bristly copper beard near Spareen's ear and said, "I'll bet you can't get Maryanka, the captain's woman. She's more stubborn and strong-willed than the usual wench."

Spareen was thoroughly enjoying himself. "Will you wager your horse against mine then?" he asked, for he secretly coveted one of the sleek Russian mounts.

"That's a fine wager for you," said Ivan, "but what would I do with that little nag you rode in on?"

"My horse may be smaller and not as fast as yours, but she's tougher. You can ride her all day and night, and feed her just the coarse grass of the steppe, and she thrives. Your big Kabarda horse would die of such treatment. Besides, my horse can do tricks. Come, I'll show you. . . ." Spareen got up and walked unsteadily toward the door. Ivan caught up with him, and together they staggered out of the house, down the steps to the street.

When they got to Rimsky's yard where the horses were penned, Spareen gave a whistle and the golden-eyes mare came trotting up to the fence. She tossed her dark mane in greeting and the moonlight picked up a glint of silver in it.

"Well, show me what she can do," said Ivan.

"How's this for a start," Spareen spoke to the mare in the old language, the horse language known only to his people. The mare backed off from the fence, then charged at it, arching up and over in a perfect leap.

"She's a lovely little thing, isn't she?" said Spareen.

"But she's barely a horse," said Ivan. "More like an oversize pony."

The mare came over and nuzzled Spareen's sleeve. He fondled her small, wedge-shaped head, pulling her forelock and tickling her ears.

"Be careful, Spareen," she said by a twitch of her nose. "Vaylance wouldn't like this."

"If you tattle on me, I'll tie a knot in your tail," he whispered.

Aloud he said, "Now, show Ivan how you can lie down," and she obediently knelt down and rolled on her side.

"Now she'll play dead." Spareen walked over to a tree that grew in the yard and picked a branch. Returning, he flicked her ears. She didn't so much as flinch, but lay as if stone. He batted at her belly. Still no response. At a soft-spoken word she scrambled to her feet again.

"All right," said Ivan. "It's a bet."

"Show me the woman," said Spareen, after he had put the mare back in the pen.

They walked back to the party a little more sober than when they had left it. When they re-entered the house, the people had redistributed so that their table was not the center of attention it had been. Ivan pointed out Maryanka, a small fine-boned woman with long black hair and pale thin face, fine as a cameo. She was sitting directly across the room from them, but try as he might, Spareen could not get her to look his way.

"I told you so," said Ivan, when he perceived that Spareen was having difficulties.

"She's a strong one," marveled Spareen. A prickle of excitement stirred the roots of his belly fur. "Yet I'll bet my brother Vaylance could get her." He secretly hoped Vaylance couldn't, but he didn't say this to Ivan.

"Vaylance the pious? Don't make me laugh!" said Ivan.

At that particular moment, Vaylance arrived back at

the party. Spareen thought he looked very tired and care-worn, as he sometimes did after a difficult healing.

"All right," said Ivan. "If Vaylance can get her to come over here, you keep your mare."

When Vaylance came up to the table, Ivan asked him about the health of the colonel, Barikoff.

"He's not doing well," said Vaylance. "But at least I've taken away some of the pain. Perhaps in a few hours we'll have some medicine for him." Vaylance pinched the bridge of Spareen's nose with fingers still hot from healing. If there had been pain, it would have been little eased.

Spareen urgently motioned is brother aside to talk to him. Vaylance, when he found out about the bet, was furious.

"You mean you've gone and wagered your sister, your horse on an outblood woman. What idiocy!" His black eyes flashed dangerously. "And I suppose you've been summoning people all night to show off, you camel's ass! You endanger my position here."

"All right, I was stupid to start it," said Spareen. "But now I've gotten into it and I don't care if I lose my horse because that woman's wolf-minded. Try yourself and see if you can get her. You're better at it than me. But remember, I saw her first."

This information caused Vaylance to pull up short in his anger. He allowed his eyes to stray over to the table where the small, fine-boned woman was sitting.

"Maryanka, the captain's woman," he mused. "Could I have overlooked her before?" He sat down at the table slowly, as if in trance, propped his chin up with one hand and concentrated on the dark-haired woman.

"So! She's even too much for your brother," said Ivan after this had gone on for a while.

Spareen and Vaylance had all but forgotten about the bet.

"She looked me in the eye once, I'm sure of it," said Spareen.

"Well, I guess you'd better close in for a better look," said Vaylance.

"You go, I'd botch it for sure."

"You saw her first," said Vaylance. "You go, but remember, if she's wolf-minded, the choice is hers, not ours."

Feeling very unsure of himself, Spareen got up and made his way over to the table where she was sitting, a little ways off from everyone else.

"Does the captain's woman drink alone?" he asked.

"I belong to no one," she replied. "I'm not a possession."

"I'm sorry," he faltered, "I didn't mean to imply that you were." She wouldn't even look at him.

"May I sit down?" he asked.

"I wish you wouldn't," she said. Still her eyes looked away.

"Very well," he said, "but you could at least look at me when you speak. It's common courtesy." Now he was sure he had her.

But when she raised her eyes and appeared to look his way, he saw that her eyes were unfocused, so that she stared through him to a place behind his back on the wall.

"An old Tartar trick!" he exclaimed. "How did you know it?"

"I know what you are," she said. "I watched you bewitching people all evening with your wild Varkela eyes."

"How do you know of the Varkela then?" he asked, for his folk kept their secret from the Cossacks.

"My grandmother taught me," she said, and then she quoted for him the rhyme that Tartars who have dealings with the Varkela teach their children:

*"To love Varkela, you must pay the cost.*
*Don't look him in the eye or you'll be lost."*

"Are you Tartar then?" he asked.

"My grandmother was. She was captured in a raid by the Cossacks." Her eyes carefully regarded the surface of the table.

"If you know of the Varkela, then you know that we are rather persistent suitors. The more you resist, the harder we try."

Anticipation stirred in him. He might lose his mare, but it would surely be worth it.

"You cannot be with someone over any long period of time and never look him in the eye," he said. "I am patient at the waiting game. You would surely lose eventually. Why not look at me now and get it over with."

She never raised her eye, and for a long time said nothing. When she finally spoke, she said:

"One thing I have heard of the Varkela is that they are an older race than we are, and have a kinship with all wild things. Some people call me the captain's woman, but it might more truly be said that he is my man, for I would rather be owner than owned. If you have any compassion for wild things, then have mercy on my untamed will. Do not command me to obey you."

He was touched by her plea and was momentarily ashamed that he had been luring people about as if he had no respect for the fact that they had wills of their own. He resolved not to compel her, but there was something he must know.

"If I promise not to summon you, will you let me look once into your eyes, that I might know what manner of creature you are?"

"What will you swear by?" she asked.

"By my father's blood," he began, regretting that he had to give an oath. "By the eight-trunked mother-tree that upholds the world, and by the gray-ghost stag sacred to my people Varkela."

He waited hopefully, but she still did not raise her eyes.

"I fear to trust you, for you are demonkind."

"Some call us that, but we are not demons. We are a people like any other people."

"There are no people like the *Children of the Night*," she said, "but I suppose I must look, trust you or not, else you'll keep me here till cockcrow, and come back the next night, and the next, until I give in. As you said, you can out wait me."

She raised dark, amber eyes and allowed him to look on them, and he saw that indeed something wild dwelt there, but he was disappointed that the wild thing was not a wolf. She had a soul-beast unusual for an outblood woman, Ranni the little musk-deer that hides in the marshes. He saw that he could summon her if he chose. But such a brave little deer she was, sitting there throwing his Varkela witching stare back at him, that he could not help but respect her. He lowered his eyes and said:

"Go with grace, little sister."

The captain's woman stood up and glided determinedly toward the door.

In his throat, Spareen felt a constriction of sadness, as he often did after such encounters. We are an old race, he thought, and we are dying out.

"You've won," he said to Ivan, when he got back to his table. He explained to Vaylance what had transpired and then, turning to the red-bearded Cossack, said, "It must be getting late for you. Hadn't we better go and collect your new horse?"

"One more before we go," said Ivan. "You must salve your loss, Spareen."

And Spareen, feeling the need of such comfort, having lost both the woman and his golden-eyes mare, drank a few more rounds for the sake of good fellowship and staggered drunkenly to the horse pens to deliver his mare into Ivan's care. Before handing over the halter rope, he taught Ivan a few words to say to her, and then whispered something in her ear. It was nearly dawn when Vaylance helped him stumble up the steps to Dr. Rimsky's cottage. They were just about to settle down to sleep when Spareen felt the familiar searing pain in his naso-dental sinuses.

"Vaylance, it's time," he said, holding his pounding temples in his hands.

"So soon?" Vaylance placed a cold finger between Spareen's eyes. Like a small, sucking mouth, the finger drew out most of the pain.

"It's time." Spareen could feel the bitter ichor of the mold leak in small golden drops from his hollow blood-teeth.

When they reached the sick room in the officers' quarters, Barikoff was twisting back on the bed in a sort of delirium, his pale, waxy face smirking in a gargoyle grimace. Rimsky was restraining the ulcerated leg in his large pink hands.

"Fever's worse," he said. "And I don't like the looks of that wound."

Spareen saw that the ulcers oozed green effluent.

"It's as bad as that other one I treated," he said to Vaylance. "I doubt this will do much good. The green pus doesn't respond to the mold-cure."

"Nevertheless, we must try," said Vaylance. "It's the only hope he has."

They drained the abscess one last time before proceeding. Spareen noted the foul smell of the green putrescence, held his breath and bit deeply into the inflamed vein of Barikoff's leg, disgorging the product of his swollen sinuses drop by drop. After a quarter of an hour, he's exhausted his supply and there was nothing to do but hope. The golden sun was just brimming over the horizon as the two brothers made their way across the foot bridge to the infirmary.

Before settling down to sleep, Vaylance brought Spareen a tin box with a fresh portion of bread dough. Spareen expelled the dregs of his sinuses into the fresh dough, then settled himself for his daytime sleep. His last waking thoughts were of the greening wound and his failure to save the Kalmuck prince Soodshi–Noyon from this same death. Then his thoughts turned toward his hunger and his longing to sink his fangs into the rich, red river of life. A small musk-deer paused a moment on the border of a marsh, then vanished to safety among the high reeds.

◆ ◆ ◆

Rimsky came early in the evening to wake them, saying, "Barikoff's fever has broken. His leg has ceased draining and begun to return to a normal color."

"Excellent," said Vaylance, sitting up. Spareen groaned and rolled over on his stomach.

He felt Vaylance shaking him but ignored it. "Too much wine," he muttered, pulling the pillow down over his head. He couldn't believe he'd affected a cure to the green-puss sickness, it must be a dream.

"Also," Rimsky continued, "Dimitry sends his apologies for abandoning you last night, and he's left a fine bottle of vodka for Spareen, although he neglected to tell me what the occasion was."

Vaylance burst out laughing and slapped his prostrate brother on the back.

"At least someone's love life is going well," he said.

Spareen belched and rolled over. His mouth tasted like the insides of his old felt boots. "What about my mare? Any word about her?"

"Oh, yes, Ivan says that fool mare dumped him three times, the third time in a gorse bush," said Rimsky.

"For shame, Spareen!" said Vaylance.

"For shame, nothing," said Spareen. "He called you a smelly goat-doctor."

"Speaking of doctors," said Rimsky, "you may someday be one, Vaylance. Barikoff was quite impressed with your healer's touch and your brother's mold-cure. He's consented to provide a grant for your continuing study of medicine."

"How wonderful," said Vaylance, jumping up to pace about the room. "Then I'll be able to continue working at the fort here with you. And perhaps Spareen could assist me." He rubbed his small hands together, restless and excited.

"I'm not so sure that's a good idea, if things like last night's episode keep occurring," Rimsky said guardedly. "There's quite a rumor going around about your brother's ability to attract women. I'm warning you, lad, those Russian boys you wish to befriend would turn on you in an instant, if they found out your true nature."

"It won't happen again," said Vaylance. "Tonight, this idiot goes back to the steppe."

"That's a fine way to show your gratitude," said Spareen, sitting up holding his head, his stomach in a state of turmoil.

"Well, you can't stay here," said Vaylance. "You take too many risks. Some superstitious Cossack might drive a stake through your heart."

Vaylance regarded Spareen sternly, as if waiting for the impact of his words to sink in, then smiled. "On second thought, maybe that's not such a bad idea. You'd make a good cadaver for my continuing study of medicine."

"I'll leave right now!" yelped Spareen. "You've convinced me." He hopped up from the bed and wobbled across the room, where he braced himself against a table to get his bearings.

"And did he really lure twenty women at once over to

his table?" asked Rimsky, his bushy gray eyebrows arched quizzically.

"Is that your scientific curiosity showing?" asked Vaylance. "Because if not, you're just as bad a gossipmonger as the rest of them."

"Purely a matter of scientific inquiry," Rimsky snapped. But he winked at Vaylance before leaving the room.

"I'm not going to cure your headache from all that wine," said Vaylance, "because you deserve it for such overindulgence."

Spareen breathed deeply a few times and quickly dragged his ungainly self over to the sink where he retched miserably, then rinsed his mouth out.

"What I'm wondering," he said when he was at last able to get his breath, "is how is it that I was able to cure the green pus sickness by the mold-cure this time?"

"I'm wondering the same thing," said Vaylance. He was staring into the tin box that held the bit of dough Spareen had brought in with him from the steppe. He took the other tin box with the dough Spareen had seeded from his sinuses the night before and held it to the light for Spareen to see. The two cultures were different, one gray-green, the other rust-brown.

"Just as our ancestors separated from humankind and became a second race, so our mold has changed from one thing to another," said Vaylance. "It's a miracle of God."

"Or a miracle of nature," said Spareen, taking the two tin boxes and closing them carefully. Two mold cures! Now he would not have to despair when a wound turned greenish under his care. His feelings of exultation were short-lived, however, for as he packed the two tin boxes in his saddlebags, his thoughts strayed to the golden-eyes mare. She was under a Cossack saddle now and it was all his fault. Something had to be done.

◆ ◆ ◆

Later that evening the golden-eyes mare saw Spareen coming toward her, dragging his saddle in one hand and rubbing his eye with the other.

"You've been fighting again," she observed.

"A little," he said, depositing the saddle on her back and tying up the cinch. He led her through the gates of the stanitza, mounted up, and turning his back on the long teeth of the Caucasus, set off for the steppe of home.

"You shouldn't be so quick-tempered," said the mare.

"I'm not quick-tempered," said Spareen. "When Ivan called me a jug-eared Tartar, I didn't hit him, and when he spat on my boots, I let it pass."

"Very commendable," said the mare.

"And when he said that my mother was a two-kopek strumpet, I didn't start anything."

"I'm proud of you for that," said the mare. "But, tell me, if your behavior was so circumspect, how did you get that lovely black eye?"

"Well, I restrained myself through it all somehow, but, little sister, when he called you a rat-tailed hinny, I felt it was a point of honor, and hit him."

"Me, a rat-tailed hinny!" neighed the mare, her ears standing straight up like the tines of a hay fork. "In that case, he got exactly what he deserved!" She switched her tail and snorted.

With pleasure he recalled how his fist had connected with a resounding crunch to Ivan's red-bearded jaw. The fellow was probably still lying there, out cold, or perhaps feeling a little weak from the two pinprick marks on the arm where Spareen had sunk his hungry were-teeth to suck a cupful into his blood-starved vessels. Spareen's hunger still pained him, but he wasn't worried. He was a skilled healer, and the nomads of the steppe would come to pay the *blood-price*.

Above him the crescent moon sailed like a golden boat upon a sea of clouds, and the steppe spread to the horizon, an ocean of billowing grass.

"And not a wolf-minded one in the bunch," he said to nobody in particular.

# LEECHCRAFT

*Leechcraft: the art of healing (archaic); also the art of blood-letting.*

—Words and Their Origins
by K.A. Haberthal

$A_t$ 1:30 A.M. MYRNA, the lab technologist, bent over the struggling patient, syringe in hand, and searched his arm for a vein. Dr. Meyer, one of the interns, held the man down as Myrna tried to tie the tourniquet.

"What's wrong with this guy?" she asked.

"DT's," said the intern.

"How come you don't tranquilize him?" asked Myrna.

"I don't like to coddle alcoholics."

Myrna found a vein in the emaciated arm and shoved the needle home, but the patient flinched away. When she pulled back the plunger, she drew no blood, only a vacuum.

"What's wrong, Vampira? Forgot to sharpen your teeth this evening?" quipped the intern.

Myrna groaned inwardly. Vampire jokes were an occupational hazard of medical technology. She withdrew the needle and tried again. This time she was successful.

"Now that's more like it," said Dr. Meyer. "I was afraid I was going to have to waste an hour, showing you how. Can we get STAT amylase, CBC and a crossmatch on that?"

Myrna injected the blood into tubes, some with anti-coagulant, some without. "Why does he need a crossmatch, STAT?" she asked. "Are you going to do surgery?" In hospital jargon STAT meant immediately.

"He needs it STAT because I ordered it STAT. Who's the doctor here, you or me?" said the intern.

"I want to know, because if I have to work my fanny off all night, I'd like to think it's for a good reason. Not just because some doctor decided to write STAT on the order."

"My, you're an assertive little lady," said Dr. Meyer. "If you must know, yes, we might have to do surgery. We think this guy has a 'hot' appendix, and the sooner you get those lab reports back, the sooner we'll know. So hustle back to the lab and get busy. You might win a date with a handsome, young doctor."

"Yuck!" said Myrna and walked away, leaving him standing there with a quizzical look on his face.

"Vampira, indeed!" she said under her breath as she stabbed at the elevator button. But when she thought about it, it made sense. A blood-drawer intent on collecting a specimen had to have a knowledge of veins and arteries, had to have a calming effect on agitated patients, and had to be able to coax blood out of the weakest, most scarred old veins; in effect, had to think somewhat like a Vampire.

When she got back to the lab, she plopped the tubes of blood into the centrifuge to spin down the clot. She threw a switch and a grumbling roar commenced as the centrifuge gained speed.

The lab was a small room crowded with machine consoles. Myrna took an anti-coagulated sample and fed it to "Clarabelle" the Coulter Counter, which slurped it up in pneumatic tubing. She watched as the little snake of red traveled up the tubing and into the reaction chambers. Winking indicated that the red and white blood cells were being counted. The printer chattered and spat out answers: Hematocrit 47.8, white cell count 16,700.

The hematocrit, the percentage of red blood cells, was normal but the white count was elevated. They would probably operate if the amylase was normal. A high amylase meant that the pancreas, not the appendix, was involved.

When the centrifuge clicked off at the end of ten minutes, Myrna reached in and slowed the spinning head with her hand to save precious minutes. She grabbed four squishy plastic bags of blood out of the refrigerator and lined them up on her desk to set up the crossmatch. Then she took serum to another console to run the amylase.

On the day shift, 30 people worked in the laboratory. On the graveyard shift, Myrna worked alone, handling the emergencies. She was a genius of time organization, as one had to be to keep up with the work of a whole hospital on a busy night. She often felt that the doctors and nurses got all the glory and that she was one of medicine's unsung heroes.

The amylase was normal. Myrna checked her crossmatch tubes and saw no clumping, a compatible reaction. She phoned Dr. Meyer with the report.

"Well, I guess you'll have to set up that crossmatch after all," he said.

"I already did," she said. "You've got four compatible units for surgery."

"My God, woman, you must be the fastest crossmatch in the West," he said, "How would you like to go out Saturday night?"

"I'm busy," said Myrna. "I've got to get my horse ready for a show."

"You mean you'd turn me down in favor of a horse?"

"Absolutely," and she hung up on him.

Shanty, a big Tennessee walking horse gelding, was the love interest in Myrna's life. His big free-swinging stride had carried her to the Plantation Walking Horse trophy last year. On the back of her tall graceful horse, Myrna felt a sense of accomplishment similar to that which she felt in her work. A lab tech working the night shift did not have much time to develop a social life, but Myrna sometimes went out of her way to avoid contact with men. And when she did go out, she was careful not to get involved. She had loved once and decided that was enough to play the fool.

She usually found herself the huntress, the predator, the seducer in her relationships. The men she ensnared on her forays into beery, cigarette-smelling nightspots were sometimes unkind. One had called her "hairy chested" after seeing the patch of silken mouse-like down that grew between her breasts. Before embracing them to that hirsute bosom, she sometimes warned, "Be careful, I bite." But after the orgasmic relief, she was always left feeling vaguely unsatisfied. Even the one man who had loved her had not fulfilled all her need, and she had backed out of the relationship feeling guilty and ungrateful. She sometimes wondered if she might be a changeling from some secret elder race.

Now that all her work was finished, she was free until the next emergency cropped up. Myrna loved the stressful nature of her work. When she had nothing to do, she would drift off into fantasies. She would imagine that she could travel back in time and bring modern medicine into a primitive setting.

Tonight she was working in an early 19th century laboratory with Robert Koch, founder of modern bacteriology. She was showing him how the growth of bread mold on a gelatin plate could inhibit the growth of bacterial colonies. Out of gratitude he pledged her his undying love and devotion (all in German) and crushed her against his bushy, bearded face, losing his *pince-nez* in the process.

Now that was silly!

She was feeling bored and hoped something would happen to get her through the rest of the night. "The sad irony of it is," she thought, "that nothing fun happens around here unless someone's dying," and with this ghoulish thought in mind she put her Bell-Boy beeper in her pocket and went downstairs to get hot brown water out of the coffee machine.

## II

*1845. Russia. The Caucasus.*

Against dark hills burst occasional red flares as Imam Shamil's troops displayed their heavy artillery against the forces of Czar Alexander II. An orange blast of cannon fire exploded in the night, and in the distance could be heard the crack of musket fire and the shouts of men. Outside a large tent, a horse-drawn wagon pulled to a halt in the mud.

"There are two more wounded out here," a voice called. "One's taken a ball in the leg and the other has a saber wound in the gut."

"Thank you," another voice answered from the depths of the tent. "Please put them on my last two beds."

In the dark, stuffy tent Vaylance knelt by a pallet on

the mud floor. One of his patients was dying. He peeled back the bloody piece of cloth and observed the neat flax string stitches that closed the wound. The man stirred in his uneasy sleep. The bleeding had stopped externally but not internally, and if it did not stop soon, he would have to resort to the dangerous process of transfusion.

"How's he doing?" asked Dr. Rimsky as he made his way among the pallets, holding a lantern high. Vaylance squinted away from the lantern. "He needs a transfusion."

The art of transfusion was seldom practiced in European medicine after the studies of Robert Boyle and others in the 17th century had shown it to be often fatal to the recipient. Vaylance, however, had learned his medical skill from a different tradition and had devised a method that worked fairly well in most cases.

"It's up to you to do it, then," said the doctor. "You have the best luck with it of anybody I've ever seen. I won't try my hand at it. Killed more than I ever saved with that method."

"Well, I guess I'd better find a donor then," Vaylance stood up. He was tall, lean and dark-haired with a sickly sallow complexion, and the most striking dark eyes—eyes that could read the soul. He staggered as he tried to stand, and Dr. Rimsky caught his arm to help him stabilize.

"I know you're not one of us, lad," said the doctor, "but even you must have your limits. You haven't been eating lately. Something is wrong."

"It bothers my conscience to feed, when you are all so sickly," said Vaylance. "When you were all fat and healthy, it was different. Now the cost is too high."

"Small good you'll be to us if you shrivel up and die of starvation," said the doctor. But he saw that his strange young friend was not to be persuaded. Vaylance, when he set his mind to follow his own inner law, was never waylaid by good advice. The fast would continue.

A year ago Vaylance had gone to Dr. Rimsky to tell him that he wished to serve in this war. Rimsky, an army surgeon, gray with age and much responsibility, had tried to discourage this young son of the Varkela from serving with the Russian soldiers.

"They would not accept you once they found you out, dear Vaylance," said the older man. "They would find out your hiding place and stake you while you slept. I cannot allow it. You must serve the Lord in some other way."

"You misunderstand my meaning," said Vaylance, fingering the wooden cross at his throat. "I would not serve as a soldier, but as a medical assistant with you. I must, for you, because you have saved me from the black-water sickness. You know my people are known for their herbal lore, leechcraft, and some for the healer's touch, and you have taught me much of the science of surgery. Let me come with you."

"The Varkela are known for other things besides their skill at healing," said Rimsky. "Even as a convert, you would be mistrusted by the men, and, besides, this is not your war, Vaylance. Your people are considered Tartar and not subject to the Czar." Rimsky hoped that Vaylance would survive the war and become a leader of his people, an ancient race which might become extinct. He had met Vaylance's father while stationed near the Caucasus. He had been surprised to find the old Varkela leechman living with a group of Kalmuck nomadic tribesman who still paid the ancient *blood-price* for his medical services.

Vaylance had not given up, however. "You forget," he said, "that I was born on Russian soil. And, remember, it has always been the custom of my people to heal the sick and wounded. When the Mongols came over the steppes and made war, did not we Varkela come in the night to ease pain and bind up wounds? All I require is that you provide me with a place to sleep, and I will keep the night watch while you work days."

"Very well," Dr. Rimsky had sighed. "You have my permission, and I will be very glad to have your assistance."

◆ ◆ ◆

The volunteer came into the dimly lighted tent and sat on the campstool. Vaylance recognized the man.

"You can't give blood again so soon, Sarnov," he said. "It takes at least a month for your body to make more. Go and send someone else."

A few minutes later another man came and presented himself. Vaylance had him lie on the cot next to the wounded man and rolled up his sleeve. He applied the tourniquet and the veins bulged like rope cords. As he worked, Vaylance sang softly the "sleeping song" of his people, which had the effect of inducing a hypnotic state in the volunteer.

With his fingers he traced the swollen veins. He could actually hear the blood hum as it pulsed through the arteries like the rushing of water in subterranean caverns. His mouth began to water as he knelt next to the cot. Gentle as a kiss, his mouth touched the exposed arm, his hollow teeth entered the vein, and a swirl of blood flowed into his mouth. A taste was enough to tell him what he wanted to know. He withdrew his mouth and licked at the wound with his thin, dog-like tongue. Saliva from his lower gland bathed the prick and stopped the bleeding.

There were four blood types Vaylance could recognize by taste: salty, more salty, bitter and slightly sweet. This was the bitter, same as his patient, and without further delay he began to set up the transfusion. He had two hollow needles, and connecting the two was a crude form of rubber tubing. In the middle of the tubing was a glass reservoir with a pair of stopcock valves, a glassblower's nightmare. Vaylance selected the proper vein on the donor's arm and inserted the upper needle, and the lower he placed into the chosen vein of his patient. Slowly the reservoir filled with the dark fluid. Vaylance reversed the stopcock and forced air into a vent on the side of the reservoir, and it slowly emptied.

Knowing that there are four major blood types was a breakthrough in the art of transfusion, but it didn't rule out all danger. There was an antibody lurking in the serum of the patient. A more sophisticated test might have detected the telltale clumping in the bottom of a test tube, but Vaylance, limited to tasting the blood, missed it completely. For this reason he did not know anything was wrong until he saw the skin of his patient go all mottled with reddish splotches. He yanked the needle from the arm, but it was too late to save the man. Hemolyzed red blood cells had already dumped a toxic load of raw hemoglobin into the system. The patient burned with fever as the night wore on. His kidneys, confronted with the hemoglobin, failed, and he entered the coma from which there was no return. As the sun came up, the surgical assistant fought his weariness and stayed near his patient's side, but abruptly he ceased to breathe, and Vaylance admitted defeat. There was nothing to do but clean all the paraphernalia and remove the corpse for burial.

Vaylance went to Dr. Rimsky's tent and woke the doctor. After telling him of the failed transfusion, he prepared to sleep. He always slept in Dr. Rimsky's tent, which was strictly off-limits to everyone except himself and the doctor. Vaylance lay on his cot thinking. Presently his breathing slowed and his pulse dropped to 20 beats per minute. He slept as only the Varkela sleep.

◆ ◆ ◆

Vaylance awoke with a start to find a crushing weight on his chest. The sun had gone down: it was time for him to work again, but something was wrong. Around him he heard the sounds of men groaning in pain. Hoofbeats approached and then receded in the distance. Then he heard a voice:

"The medical tent's been hit! Give us a hand."

Vaylance struggled with the weight on his chest and found it was a dead man.

"Over here!" he called to the voices.

Someone was moving the heavy tent cloth, and then strong hands reached in and pulled him from the wreckage. Vaylance then helped his rescuer, a large man in an ill-fitting black infantryman's uniform, to clear away the remains of the tent and find the wounded men.

"Shamil's broken through the front here," said the burly soldier as he hefted a stump-legged patient.

"Go and find me a wagon to move the wounded," Vaylance ordered.

Vaylance began to check his patients, who were lying scattered about on the muddy ground. Several of them had died, perhaps from shock or suffocation when the tent was hit. A cannon ball whistled overhead and burrowed into the clay of a nearby embankment. Suddenly he realized Dr. Rimsky was missing. He blundered back into the tent and floundered amid the fallen poles and tent cloth until he found the doctor lying face-down. He was wet all over and the smell of fresh blood hung heavy on the night air. Vaylance turned Rimsky over and saw where a tent pole had slashed an artery in his arm. He found the doctor's medical kit and began to work, quickly removing the pole and applying a pressure bandage to the wound. He prayed that the bleeding would stop.

Then he heard the approach of wagon wheels. The big soldier was back with two others, and they began to load the wounded into the cart. Vaylance lifted the doctor gingerly and placed him in the wagon. Then he climbed up and stayed at the doctor's side as the wagon creaked slowly over the soggy ground. By two hours past midnight they had reached an encampment of supply wagons.

A tall grimacing officer with epaulets on his shoulders approached the wagon on horseback.

"We are the Fourth Medical Unit," said Vaylance, "or rather what's left of it. The doctor is wounded. I am the surgical assistant."

The officer nodded and called to some men by the supply depot. In an hour they had the tent up and had made the patients as comfortable as possible. There were six patients left, including Dr. Rimsky. As Vaylance made his rounds, he was encouraged to see that one of his patients with the leg amputated at the knee was doing well. The man's fever had responded to an infusion of willow leaves, and the stump was healing without infection.

Vaylance was worried about Dr. Rimsky, however, and he decided to re-dress the wound. But when he set the new bandage in place, he saw where the blood still oozed to darken the fresh white cloth. And he realized his hunger. The nearness of blood was beginning to affect him again. He hastily finished the dressing and stepped out of the tent to gaze at the moon. The moon waned in the eastern sky, a thin scimitar of light. In a few nights would come the dark of the moon, the blood-moon, as his people called it.

◆ ◆ ◆

The Varkela had originally been horse nomads of the Eurasian steppes, wandering from tribe to tribe, exchanging their skill at healing for the *blood-price*. For centuries they had survived, one here, a few there, in close association with humankind, yet always a race apart, a secret brotherhood. According to oral tradition, they had served in the legions of Attila the Hun around 400 A.D., and when Batu Khan, grandson of Genghis, invaded the Russian frontier, he found tribes that still employed the services of the old Varkela leechman. By Vaylance's time they had mostly died out or had interbred with humankind to the extent that the old genetic traits had been diluted out. One occasionally ran across Varkela characteristics among the Circassian people of the Caucasus or their Tartar neighbors on the steppes. Every now and then, a youth would have those dark, seductive eyes that seemed to exert so much power over the beholder. Or there would be a Tartar brave with such uncanny ability to train horses that people would say of him, "He speaks the horses' language." Blood-need was of course extremely uncommon. One Circassian folktale tells of the wolf-minded Tartar maid who lures a Cossack youth away into the night to drink his blood.

The Varkela had left their imprint on the Slavic racial memory in the form of Vampire stories.

By their strange nocturnal habits and their state of daylight dormancy, they had been regarded as "undead," the nosferatu. The old Greek word for Vampire, "Vrkolakas," may be a corruption of Varkela, the *Children of the Night*.

◆ ◆ ◆

As the gray dawn appeared, Vaylance left the medical tent and sought out the officer he had seen earlier. He found the man sitting on a wooden crate, cleaning a small flintlock handgun that rested on his knee. The officer forced a wet rag down the small bore with a straight alder stick, and with loving hands he polished the smudges of powder burn from the browned metal flashpan. His well-fed gray mare stood patiently tied to the supply wagon. It raised its head and swiveled its ears toward Vaylance, making a barely audible nicker. Vaylance scratched the animal's poll.

"A fine animal you've got here," he said. Then he proceeded with his lie:

"I must go to a nearby village and seek sheeting to make bandages. Could you please assign someone to stay with the wounded until I return?" He hoped this would be a good excuse to sneak away and take his daytime sleep. He no longer had Dr. Rimsky to explain away his odd habits. The taciturn officer nodded and continued his polishing. Vaylance turned to take his leave, then added:

"By the way, your horse has a stone wedged in her left fore hoof."

◆ ◆ ◆

The road to the village branched, and Vaylance took the less traveled fork. Soon he was ascending a small hillock that was heavily wooded. The increasing light made it hard for him to see, and he welcomed the shadow of the trees. He found a dense thicket where he hoped he would not be discovered, and burrowing into the underbrush, he flattened the grasses and made a place to lie down. He drowsed, pondering his troubles. He might have to transfuse Dr. Rimsky, his dearest friend, yet he feared to take the risk without further knowledge. He would have to risk dreamwalk to find the answer. The trouble with dreamwalking was that he never knew where he might end up, and he needed someone else to help him do it, but it was the only course open to him. With resolution, Vaylance stopped breathing, slowed his heart and loosed his soul into the void.

He felt as if he were lifted up above the gently rolling hills of the Russian countryside, and he could see the grove where he slept far below. Then the landscape shimmered and disappeared, and in its place came the flat, dry grasslands of the open steppe. A yurt, a tent-like dwelling, stood like a bump in the flat plain, its felt cloth sides rippling in the wind. A few scruffy horses were grazing nearby, and a two-humped Bactrian camel lay sunning itself, its face toward the wind. The surroundings shimmered again, and Vaylance found himself inside the arched cane poles of the yurt. On a wicker couch lay an old man, whose leathern Tartar features, windburned and ancient, did not change, but acknowledged the presence in the yurt.

"My son, do you dreamwalk?" asked the old man.

"My father, I greet thee from the void," answered Vaylance. "I feel myself being pulled forward in the river of time, and I need your help." Vaylance explained his predicament to his father.

"The last time something like this happened," said Freneer, the father, "you almost brought back that unclean woman as your blood-love. You know I am against these outblood liaisons of yours. Favarka's been dead a long time, and I think you should take another mate. I am seeking a Varkela wife for you. You must consider, Vaylance, that we are dying out as a race; if the young men do not produce offspring, the 'old knowledge' will die with us."

"I don't intend to let you breed me like a horse, Father," said Vaylance. "Right now marriage is far away from my thoughts. I must find a way to save Dr. Rimsky."

"And yet you let that Russian doctor study you like some species of beetle—but I know he is your friend, and I will help you—but you must promise to choose some wolf-minded girl, just as I chose your mother Odakai."

◆ ◆ ◆

Vaylance remembered his mother, a Varkela woman who had left the steppes to live in Moscow, where she practiced as a medium and spiritual healer under the name of Anna Varkeerovna. He had lived with her until he was about thirteen, learning French and English in the drawing-room society of Moscow, and then she had taken him back to the steppe to study leechcraft with his father. One night on their journey to the steppes she had come across a wolf-cub which she had picked up and carried for a while across her saddle bow, saying to her young son: "This is the soul-beast of your blood-love, Vaylance." His parents insisted on a pedigree.

◆ ◆ ◆

"Very well, a wolf-minded girl," Vaylance agreed, "but in my own time, Father, and in my own way."

"Well, then," said the old leechman, "let us begin." He took his staghorn rattles from the altar and sat cross-legged on the rug. Beating the horns together, he began to croon softly in the old language.

Vaylance sat on the rug opposite his father and concentrated on Dr. Rimsky. Gradually the singing got softer and Vaylance felt time, like a river, flowing around him. He let go and drifted with the current. Then he did not hear the singing anymore; in its stead came a sound like rushing water in his ears. He entrusted himself to the forward dream and waited.

III

Myrna sat up with a start. A face at the blood bank window was enough to jolt her from her reverie.

"Got a live one for you down in admitting!" said the intern, offering Myrna tubes of blood. "Not bleeding now but he seems to have lost a lot somewhere along the way. Hematocrit of sixteen. Dressed like he was going to a costume party. Also he didn't have any I.D. So we just gave him a number. And if you haven't already guessed, we want it STAT."

Myrna fed a sample to "Clarabelle" and got a reading: Hematocrit 15.9 percent, white cell count 4000.

"He won't live long at that rate," she said, as she plopped the tube into the centrifuge to spin. She was most concerned about the low hematocrit, the volume of red blood cells expressed as a percentage. Normal for an adult male was 45 percent. At 15.9 this patient wasn't doing at all well.

When the centrifuge stopped turning, Myrna retrieved the tube of blood, separated the serum from the clot and prepared to type the sample. She added typing serum, spun the tubes and frowned.

"Damn it! He doesn't type," she said, looking at the mixed-field agglutination in the A tube. "Must be a weak subtype of A; either that, or someone's been mixing A and O together." Uncertainty about a blood type was about the worst problem a tech could have when blood was needed for a transfusion.

Myrna had seen a reaction like this only twice before. Once had been when a patient of type O blood had been mistakenly given type A. The other had been when she had been new on the job, just out of training school. An intern had brought her a specimen to type for a "friend." She had at first been puzzled until she looked at the name on the tube: "I. M. Nosferatu." Then she had to laugh. Someone was pulling her leg. The intern had mixed A and O together as they might be expected to occur in the stomach of the fictitious Mr. Nosferatu. It was the ultimate vampire joke.

The man would have to be transfused with such a low hematocrit. So Myrna decided the best thing to do would be to collect a fresh specimen and repeat the tests. Hopefully someone had made a mistake the first time. She filled a tray with the tools of her trade: sterile needles encased in plastic, rubber tourniquet, vacutaner tubes, cotton swabs, alcohol and skin tape. Then she took the elevator to the intensive care unit.

The sweet, sickly odor of the patients hit her as she walked into the ICU. The most critical patients lay in full view of the nursing station, looking like a row of strange vegetables planted in a garden of wires and plastic tubing. The heart monitors peeped every few seconds, and electric recording devices hummed in the background.

"Hi, Rose," she said to the older woman at the nursing station. "I need a new specimen on your Mr. Number 3489."

"First door on your left," said Rose, "and good luck. I don't think he's got any blood left."

She had expected him to be unconscious when she entered the room, but he was awake and looking at her. He looked to be about thirty, with a shaggy crop of black hair and the most striking dark eyes that glowed faintly as if there were light inside of him. There was something too intimate about looking into those eyes.

And then Myrna had one of those occasions that people in her family called "second sight." She seemed to see a woman, wearing a Cossack's baggy clothing and a fur cap, sitting astride a horse facing into the wind. In the crook of her arm was a wolf cub. The woman stroked the cub and turned her head toward Myrna and smiled at her with those same large dark eyes. She spoke a few words and then the image faded. Myrna realized she was standing there staring at the patient, who regarded her with a whimsical smile.

"This must be an English hospital and you are the leech," he said. He had an accent, although she couldn't place it, and she instinctively knew that he used the word "leech" in its oldest sense, the archaic term for "doctor."

"I suppose you could call me a leech of sorts," she

said, "but I'm not a doctor, I'm a medical technologist. And this isn't England. You're in America, friend."

"America!" he exclaimed. "I thought there were only wild Indians and revolutionaries living there. What year is this?"

"Nineteen seventy-nine," she said.

"My God!" he said. "When I went to sleep it was 1845."

"What did you do, fall asleep in a time machine? Or are you Rip Van Winkle?"

"Neither, I hope," he said. "If things are what I think they are, then I'm dreamwalking, and I'm not really here."

"We'll see about that," she said tying the tourniquet around his arm and swabbing vigorously with alcohol. She stuck the needle into his arm and pushed the vacutaner down snugly, breaking the vacuum. Blood was sucked into the tube. Suddenly he clenched his arm, causing the needle to pop out leaving a little trail of red. His hand closed over her wrist tightly.

"Do not take from me, little blood-thief," he said. "I don't have enough to give."

"You don't understand," she said. "I must test your blood for the right type and do a crossmatch. Then they will give you a transfusion because you have lost much blood."

"I have not lost any," he said. "But I have need of it. I have not taken blood in a month." After divulging this bit of information he stared at the few drops of blood in the tube. Perplexed, he said, "Perhaps I'm really here and Rimsky is over one hundred years dead." He lay back on the pillow and closed his eyes. He seemed to be concentrating on something very far away. For a moment she seemed to see his image fade before her eye so that she thought she could see through him, and then he was back, solid as before.

"It's all right," he said. "I can still hear my father's voice if I listen."

Something very odd was going on here. She wrinkled her brow and studied him for a moment. Then businesslike and efficient, she retied the tourniquet.

"I don't know what's happening," she said, "but whatever it is, my time-travelling friend, you had better give me some blood so I can get back to the lab, or you are going to be one sick turkey." She tried to maintain a calm appearance as she bent over him to obtain the specimen.

◆ ◆ ◆

There was something about this woman that attracted Vaylance. For a brief moment, when he had looked into her eyes, he thought he had seen the "look of the wolf." And there was something else. Beneath the civilized odor of cologne and talc, he detected a fragrance, imperceptible to human-kind, of something definitely feral, as wild and sweet as the crushed leaves of his medicinal herbs, and this excited him. It called to mind a verse from one of the great Varkela love poems. He converted it into English in his mind and came up with: "Ah, woman, the scent of thy wolvish cunt hath turned my head." It was intended as a compliment, but was definitely not the sort of thing one said to an English-speaking lady in his time; so he kept it to himself.

As she bent over him, he observed that her hair was piled up on her head and held in place by a clip. The nape of her neck was lovely and vulnerable in the halflight, and he felt a strong urge to press his lips to her inviting throat and sink his cat-like teeth into the pulsing artery. Thinking this way caused him to have an erection, and he smiled inwardly at his attempt to stifle the impulse. This Christianity that he practiced was more difficult than the shamanistic religion of Freneer, his father. One of the saints had called the body "brother ass," an appropriate term for his, as it sometimes went stubbornly astray.

She finished drawing the blood sample and left the room, taking her fragrance with her. If she gave him blood, he would have to give her something in return. He knew some members of his race, especially those in the Balkan countries, stole blood like vile insects, giving neither love nor leechcraft in return.

It had been a long time since he had shared blood-love with a woman. Service in the Czar's army did not provide many opportunities. He had counted himself lucky when at the age of 17 he had won the love of Favarka, a full-blooded Varkela. Women were so rare that he'd shared her with another older man, according to their custom, but she'd called him "favorite." She was ten years dead, but he sometimes thought of her and the times he had laid his head on the soft fur between her breasts. He still carried the small scars where Favarka in her passion had marked him hers with love bites.

◆ ◆ ◆

Back at the lab, Myrna fussed with her test tubes and got the same frustrating results. Holding the tubes up to the light, she saw little red flecks in the typing serum.

"This will have to do, I guess," she said.

Dr. Meyer was waiting at the window, impatiently drumming his fingers along the countertop.

"You'll have to sign for this one," said Myrna.

"That bad, huh?" he said.

"He doesn't type," she said. "I called my supervisor and she said give O-negative packed cells. At least he doesn't have any serum antibodies that I can detect."

"Maybe it's a hypoimmune response," said Dr. Meyer. "You know, that guy is weird. 'Crit of 16, and he sits up in bed asking me questions all night. I'm surprised he can move his mouth, let alone sit up. You'd better loan

him one of your books on blood-banking. He's asking
things that are over my head."

♦ ♦ ♦

At 5:00 a.m. when things had quieted down, Myrna
was washing out the tubing on the auto-analyzer. She
was finished and just about to get a cup of coffee, when
she heard it. She did not exactly "hear" it, for there was
no sound, but the definite words came to her: "Come to
me," they said.

She got her coffee and sat down at the lab bench to
think this over.

"Come to me."

It was a voice inside her head pleading subtly but insis-
tently. *It was him.* It had to be him.

Her curiosity compelled her sufficiently that when
Ernie the security guard came by, she asked him to
watch the phone while she went upstairs.

The ICU was quiet except for the beep-beep of the
heart monitors. When she entered the room, her patient
was lying back on the bed with a smile on his face and
a little white tooth projected over his lower lip. He had
taken the IV needle from his arm and placed the tubing
over one of his teeth. The blood bag, hung on a rack
overhead, was emptying visibly. He seemed quite pleased
with himself.

"You didn't come right away," he said. "That means
you are somewhat wolf-minded—sit here." He pointed
to the bed. His voice was quiet, but she could feel the
command in it. And she felt an overwhelming desire to
obey his commands, especially when she looked into
those dark, seductive eyes. Somehow she resisted: he
would not have fun at her expense. What is happening,
she thought, is that he is trying to control my mind. With
an effort, she raised her eyes from his.

"Suppose I refuse," she said.

His spell was broken, but he didn't look at all unhappy about it; in fact, quite the contrary.

"You know, you're one of the few people who can do that?" he said. "This is even better than I'd hoped." His eyes appraised her carefully, with a certain longing, laced with self-confidence.

She detested his smugness. "You'd better get that needle back in your arm before a nurse catches you."

He heaved a languorous sigh and winked at her.

She shivered and walked determinedly from the room. Halfway down the hall, she heard it again: "Come back."

*The hell I will*, thought Myrna.

"Please?"

*No!*

He was ecstatic to think that he could find a wolf-minded girl in this place.

◆ ◆ ◆

At 8:00 a.m. Myrna went home from the hospital. She unlocked the door to her small apartment, crossed the room and turned on the television to keep her company. A blink of light, and the Morning Show came on. A psychiatrist was being interviewed about the effect of modern technology on the psyche. "We may find," he was saying, "that man needs mythology more than all the conveniences of our modern age." Myrna left the voices mumbling behind her, as she took the few steps to the kitchen. She stooped to open the small refrigerator that fitted under the counter and peered among the cottage cheese cartons and plastic-wrapped packages. She selected a package of two-day-old chicken, removed a drumstick, and shut the door.

Her small breakfast finished, she turned off the TV and opened the bedroom door. In one corner stood a clothes hamper stuffed to overflowing, and in the middle of the room lay a mattress under a heap of blankets.

Beside it were piled the books she was currently reading. There was also the letter from Terry, in which he complained of her inability to say the word "love." The most she would say to someone she felt close to was, "I care for you." She had written back to him: "There is something wild in me that won't be caged by love."

Along one wall of her room was a bookcase that reached from floor to ceiling. She went to the wall and searched among the titles. Following one row with her finger, she stopped on *The Vampire, His Kith and Kin*, by Montagu Sommers. She tossed it on the bed and went to the bureau and opened the top drawer. She searched a while among the lipstick cases, pill bottles, and mismatched socks. It wasn't there. She pulled open the next drawer and sorted around the underwear until she found the little wooden jewelry box. Inside the box, tangled in a mass of neck chains and a string of pearls, she found the object of her search, a tiny silver cross, given to her when she was a little girl by her grandmother. She had never worn it, but she put it around her neck now. Then she began to undress. Removing her white nylon pants, she put on her flannel nightgown, rearranged the blankets, and settled into her nest to read. Eventually she fell mid-paragraph into a restless sleep.

◆ ◆ ◆

The use of the cross as a religious symbol predates Christianity, going back as far as neolithic times. It was usually a glyph for the axe or hammer and, as such, signified power. To the Teutonic tribes of northern Europe, it represented the hammer of Thor. In the Shamanistic tradition of Eurasia it was Skaldi's hammer, the sun's hammer. To the Varkela, *Children of the Night*, the sun was viewed as an ancient enemy. For them the idea of a bright, sunny day had the same connotation as we might attribute to the phrase "dark of the moon." The sun hammer was regarded as a bad omen, as is echoed in the Varkela curses: "May the sun hammer smite thee," or "May the sun strike you blind." As a Christian symbol, the cross was supposed to ward off the devil, and so by converse logic the Varkela were regarded as "demonkind" because they avoided it.

◆ ◆ ◆

That evening Myrna went early to the hospital. She went to the intensive care unit and inquired about the progress of her patient.

"He had a code 99 this morning, cardiac arrest," Rose reported. "They had to resuscitate him. Lucky they caught him when they did or he would have been gone."

Nervously Myrna entered the room and stood inside the doorway watching the figure on the bed. In her lab coat pocket she fingered her silver crucifix. He was sitting up in bed and he smiled when he recognized her.

"A person could get killed in a place like this," he said. "This morning when I was almost asleep, they came in and jolted me right out of it with that horrible shock machine."

"You're lucky," she said. "They could have decided you were dead and sent you to pathology for an autopsy. Then you would be all cut up and placed in little bottles by now."

"I see this age has its share of barbarous customs," he said.

Myrna took a step into the room, fumbling with the object in her pocket.

"You're a vampire, aren't you?" she said, stopping at what she hoped was a safe distance from the bed.

"I'm not a corpse come back to life, if that's what you mean," he said. "But I am Varkela, which is probably the source of all those silly legends."

♦ ♦ ♦

Vaylance eyed her pocket mistrustfully, thinking it must contain a small hand pistol. When outbloods began using the word "vampire" it usually meant trouble, and only a fool would stick around trying to argue about technical differences. Therefore he was quite relieved when she took a small crucifix out of her pocket and extended her arm triumphantly in his direction.

Aha, he thought, someone comes to smite me down with the sun's hammer. He decided to have a little fun with her. Shrinking down in the bedclothes and feigning terror, he watched as she advanced in somnambulistic grandeur. When she was within range and the little cross dangled in front of his nose, he reached out and took it from her hand. An impudent grin spread across his face.

"Thank you," he said, "but as you can see, I already have one," and he pulled at the chain around his neck, bringing his own hand-carved cross into view.

Crestfallen, Myrna sat down on the bed, her mouth gaping.

"Little blood-thief," he said, "if you only knew how funny you looked just then."

"But I thought . . ." she began.

"I can be a Christian like anyone else," he said.

She didn't seem to hear him. She was still recovering from the shock.

"Hello," he waved a hand in front of her face. "You of all people don't have to be afraid of me. A wolf-minded girl can defend herself. I won't bite you or whatever it is you are afraid of."

He was glad when he saw the wolvish look return to her eyes, but now she regarded him with such a stern expression that he stopped smiling. She was angry with him.

"I suppose you think this is a soup kitchen, where you

can come for a free meal," she said. "I work hard to crossmatch blood for *sick* people. I'll have you know blood costs sixty dollars a pint, if you're interested. If you're hungry, go find someone who's healthy and bite them on the neck!"

He felt ashamed to have taken blood without payment.

"You don't need to haggle the price of blood with me," he said. "I know it comes dear, and I will find some way to repay, but right now I need your help."

He began to explain to her about the war in 1845, about his work in the medical tent, and about his dearest friend Dr. Rimsky who lay dying in another time. He watched her face for signs of comprehension. At first she raised a cynical eyebrow at his outpouring, but he rushed onward with his story, hoping to convince her by his urgency if not with logic. Soon her skepticism was replaced by doubt. She began to ask questions and to demand explanations on certain points. Eager to sway her his way, he supplied detail upon detail. Finally, as the torrent of his rhetoric abated, he thought he saw just the barest glimmer of belief in her eyes.

When he finished, Myrna was quiet for a moment. Then she said, "You know, you're not such a bad sort, and I'm half persuaded that you're telling the truth, but you make a horrible first impression. If you wanted my help, why didn't you ask me, instead of going through all that stupid 'come to me' business? You scared me half to death."

"I'm sorry about that," he said. "I was only thinking of myself. You see, I have not shared blood-love with anyone for a long time and your response was so typically Varkela, that I forgot for a moment that you are an out-blood and do not understand. Most of humankind cannot resist the 'call' and will come to us when summoned, but those who resist, the wolf-minded ones, are those we prefer to mate with, for they usually have some Varkela ancestry. But there are also wolf-minded outbloods here and there, and we also marry with them, because full-blood Varkela women are subject to an illness, and thus are very rare."

"It must be a sex-linked genetic defect," said Myrna.

"A what?"

"Never mind," she said. "Listen, if I'm going to help you, we're going to have to get you out of this place. Otherwise they'll keep trying to start your heart every morning, and you'll never get any rest."

"That's not the only thing," said Vaylance. "These doctors think I'm human. They are planning to transfuse me again tonight to raise my what-you-call-it."

"Hematocrit."

"Right. But I'm Varkela and don't need as much. It would be a waste of good blood and might even make me ill."

"I saw your chart and your 'crit is only eighteen. No doctor is going to sign your release," she said. "I can get your clothes from admitting and you can come and stay at my place for a while, but I don't know how to smuggle you past the nurses' station."

"That's no problem to me," he said, and so saying, he concentrated for a few minutes, and his image faded from view. Then he was back again. "I would have done it sooner, but I had no place to go."

"I have to go to work now," said Myrna, checking her watch. "But if you can slip past the nurses and meet me down at the lab, I'll have your things. I can teach you about transfusion, and maybe we can rig up a sort of crossmatch that would work back in 1845."

◆ ◆ ◆

About 2:30 a.m. Ernie, the security guard, came by the lab to tell Myrna that one of the patients was missing from the ICU and that she should keep an eye out for him. After he left, Vaylance materialized behind the filing cabinet.

"I wish I knew that trick," said Myrna. "I'd vanish every time my supervisor came around with a stool specimen to analyze."

"It's merely an illusion of the dreamwalk," he said. "One shouldn't do it too often. It expends a frightful lot of energy."

Myrna seated Vaylance at the lab bench and prepared to teach him immuno-hematology.

"The four major blood groups, A, B, AB, and O, are probably what you are able to distinguish by taste," she said. "We differentiate them by adding typing sera to the blood specimen." She showed him how the blue serum precipitated group A; the yellow, group B. For type AB, both the blue and yellow serum precipitated and for type O, neither of them did.

"The next thing you have to worry about are antibodies," she said. "A person with type A has Anti-B antibodies in his or her serum; this is why you can't give type-B blood to a type-A person. A type-B person has Anti-A; therefore, you can't give type-A to a B person. A type-O person has both Anti-A and Anti-B; therefore, you can't give type A or B to an O person; but type O is sometimes called the "universal donor" because you can give it to type A, B and AB persons because they don't have an Anti-O in their serum."

"Now you've got me really confused," said Vaylance. "I'll never be able to remember all that."

"You won't have to," said Myrna, "because I am going to teach you a simple crossmatch technique, which should rule out some of the dangers." She then took two different blood specimens and separated the serum from the cells. Next, using a porcelain slide, she mixed the donor cells with the patient serum on one side, and the patient cells with the donor serum on the other.

"If either mixture reacts, then you know that the donor is the wrong blood type, or that he has an antibody against the patient, making an incompatible crossmatch."

She showed Vaylance how to let the blood clot and take off the serum, and how to mix serum and cells on the slide to make what she called a "major" and a "minor" crossmatch.

"It's not perfect," said Myrna, "but it will pick out a few antibodies and prevent errors in typing."

Most of the rest of the night they talked about blood and transfusions and antibodies. She asked him how drinking the blood could raise his hematocrit, and he explained that the blood didn't go into his stomach, but that most went through valves in his hollow teeth and directly into his bloodstream. The serum antibodies were apparently filtered out somewhere in the process. She theorized that he probably had a deficiency of rubriblasts in his bone marrow, which caused the blood-need he felt from time to time. She was surprised to discover that a "vampire" needed only two pints of blood in the course of a month and could subsist on small amounts taken from many, healthy, sleeping donors. Vaylance revealed that he had two kinds of saliva: from the lower gland, a rapid clotting agent, and from the upper gland, an anticoagulant. Myrna was fascinated and asked if she could take samples.

"You're as bad as Dr. Rimsky," said Vaylance. "He experiments with my spit on men, rats, and horses. I've spent hours drooling into bottles for the furtherance of science."

◆ ◆ ◆

Vaylance noticed that during their long conversation, she seemed to avoid any topics of a personal nature. There was a certain aloofness or distance that she tried to maintain. And he was reminded of how he had been after Favarka's death, the withdrawal from life and the inward nursing of pain. He was not sure how to broach the subject. So he decided on the bold, blunt approach.

"Have you ever loved anyone, Myrna?" he asked.

She pondered this for a long time and then answered: "Yes, once a long time ago."

"And he hurt you?" asked Vaylance gently.

"How did you know?"

"I don't know, I just sense it," he said.

There was a long silence, punctuated by the clicking of the peristaltic pump on the autoanalyser and the ringing of a distant telephone.

Finally he said, "And you've never allowed yourself to love anyone since." It was a statement of fact, not a question.

"Does that show too?" she asked defensively.

"It does," he said. "Don't you know that if you refuse to love, the wound may heal over on the surface, but inside an abscess grows, poisoning you from within?"

"Love is an illusion," said Myrna. "Two people come together to satisfy their own needs. The secret lies in not caring too much. That way you don't get hurt when they leave you."

He knew that this cynical answer was just her defense against deeper feelings, but it angered him, moving him to say:

"But in that way you defeat your own purpose. You hurt people and use them and drive them away. Don't you see that if you continue in that way, you will become more of a vampire than I am?"

He saw a flash of anger in her eyes, and then she looked away, biting her lower lip. He saw that his words had had an effect: she wept silently.

Well and good, he thought, she will learn to care again. He reached out and put an arm around her shoulders.

"Heal thee, heal thee," he said after the custom of his people.

When she had dried her eyes and regained some of her composure, she said, "It's not fair of you to knock down a person's defenses like that."

"It's fair if my intentions are honorable, which they are," he said.

She had to laugh at "honorable intentions."

"Now I really believe you are from the nineteenth century," she said. "Welcome to the age of noncommitment, Vaylance."

◆ ◆ ◆

At 8:00 a.m. Myrna took him home with her. At first he balked at the "horseless carriage," her Volkswagen Superbeetle, but she finally persuaded him to get into the metal contraption. At her apartment she prepared him a place to sleep on cushions on the living room floor. Then she went to take her own daytime rest.

She awoke to hear music. He had found her old guitar and retuned it to resemble some instrument familiar to him. He strummed a minor chord and sang in his own language. It had the sound of cold wind howling across open plains.

"What is that you're singing?" she asked.

He translated for her:

*"The dun mare has died,*
*Little sister of the wind*
*She wanders the pasture of the spirit world.*
*I hear her neigh sometimes*
*When the north wind blows."*

It moved her to confess to him. "I have a horse."

"Really?" he said. "You must take me out to meet him

tonight before I leave. But first I want to hear you sing for me."

She didn't like to think of his leaving. The more she got to know him, the more she felt he was the sort of man that she had always hoped to meet. She took the guitar from him and retuned it, and played an old Scottish ballad, a favorite of hers called "The Waters of Tyne."

> "Oh, I cannot see my love if I would dee.
> The waters of Tyne stand between him and me.
> And here I must sit with a tear in my ee,
> All sighin' and sobbin' my true love to see."

Except that when she sang it her tongue stumbled so that it came out "the waters of time."

◆ ◆ ◆

She took him out to the stable where she kept Shanty, her horse. Crickets were singing in the warm night, when they arrived, and Shanty trotted up to the fence to greet them, pushing his nose into Myrna's pocket to beg for sugar. Vaylance scratched Shanty's neck and then bent, sliding his hand down a foreleg to check the hoof.

"You'd better be careful. He's fussy about his feet," warned Myrna. She thought of the farrier, whom Shanty had chased out of the barn. The man refused to go near Shanty now unless the horse was hobbled.

Shanty, however, made no trouble, and at a soft-spoken word picked up his feet and allowed them to be examined.

"He isn't usually like this with strangers," said Myrna. "He's really taken to you."

Vaylance took hold of the horse's mane and vaulted up onto his back. Shanty made a half rear and pivoted, galloped to the far end of the field and came back at an easy lope. Vaylance bounced down next to her again.

"You can ride a strange horse without saddle or bridle!" exclaimed Myrna.

"Only to show off for you," he said. "Actually, I am not that good. Back home I could introduce you to some real riders. When you tell a Russian boy that he rides like a Cossack, he takes it as a compliment, but to Varkela it is an insult."

◆ ◆ ◆

When they got back to the apartment they were hungry. Vaylance insisted on cooking for her.

"It is a custom of ours. I haven't prepared food for a woman in a long time. It would give me pleasure," he said.

They searched in the refrigerator and found lamb chops. Vaylance, as he set about to cook, consumed a quart of milk, explaining that on the steppes he had lived mostly on mare's milk. Myrna showed him how to work the electric stove and then found a snack for herself as she awaited the results of his experiment.

"What's that funny stuff you're eating?" he asked. "Surely that can't be good for you."

"Coca-Cola and potato chips. I eat them all the time."

"Ugh!" he said.

"What's wrong with it?" said Myrna, knowing full well but desiring to provoke him a little. They had been having contests of the will all day. It was some sort of Varkela custom having to do with courtship or flirting.

"If you were my blood-love, I'd make you eat lots of green, leafy foods, bran meal and meat," he said.

"Why?"

"So my love wouldn't weaken you, and your blood would grow back rich and strong. I'd not have it said that my woman faints. And of course you would have to eat lots of karacheer."

"What's that?"

"Jerked goat's liver."

"Bleccchhh!"

"If you wouldn't, I'd force it down your throat!"

"The hell you would!" she said.

He engaged her eyes and tried to stare her down. She felt the force of his will as he tried to "Call" her to him. She thought a fierce, sharp thought that sent him reeling backward.

"Ow, you *are* wolf-minded. Now you've gone and given me a headache just as Favarka used to do."

It was fun, but it made him look at her throat with such longing.

"You will eventually yield to me, won't you?" he asked hopefully. "It's not fair for you to be so good at the teasing game if you don't intend to yield."

"Wait and see," she said. She seemed to have the upper hand and she was enjoying it.

After dinner she had to admit he was a very good cook.

◆ ◆ ◆

His presence had stimulated Myrna into a lovely fantasy. She had an idea:

"I wish I could dreamwalk and go back with you. I think I'd like helping you in the medical tent. I know first aid and I could teach you a lot about modern medicine."

Vaylance was surprised. He had been wishing he had more time with her. Then perhaps it might have worked.

"We don't know each other well enough," he said. "To dreamwalk requires love and trust in your guide. It can be dangerous."

"We could at least try," she said.

He tried half-heartedly to dissuade her. He really

wished it could be so. Finally he agreed to try. He sat her in a chair and stared into her eyes, trying to put her into the proper trance. But she resisted. He could see that she didn't mean to, but she couldn't help it. The wolf in her that so strongly attracted him fought against him now.

"Keep trying," she insisted. "I feel something beginning to happen."

Carefully he tried to coax her soul into the void. Finally he seemed to be succeeding. She slumped forward in her chair.

♦ ♦ ♦

Myrna found herself inside a long, dark tunnel. She moved toward gray light in the distance until she felt grass under her feet, and, looking up, she saw the night sky, a panoply of stars. In the distance a rider approached over the steppe. No sound came to her from the horse's hooves, only the small ringing of tiny bells. She could see the rider clearly now, outlined against the starry mist, a woman clad in baggy trousers wearing a fur cap. A loose Tartar jacket enclosed her arms, which held a small wolf cub. The sturdy horse of the steppes came to a halt before Myrna, shaking its mane with a sprinkle of wind chimes. The fierce, dark-eyed woman offered the cub to Myrna, who cradled it in her arms. No word was spoken. The rider spurred her mount and cantered away, making no sound except the jingle of tiny bells.

Myrna looked at the small wolf and thought she saw sentience begin to glow redly in the depth of its eyes. Abruptly its countenance changed so that it was no longer a cub, but the wizened face of a small demon.

"Are you then one of the chosen?" it asked of her.

Myrna screamed and flung down the cub. Where it fell the ground split open in a great rent. Something made a scratchy noise deep in the dark hole, and then

Myrna saw it, a giant centipede-like creature with many-jointed legs. It began to come toward her. She turned and fled. As she ran, she could hear the gnashing of chitinous jaws just behind her. Then she was in the tunnel again, which seemed to wind on forever as the thing gained on her. Just as a whip-like antenna snaked out to touch her shoulder, she woke up sobbing in Vaylance's arms.

"I was afraid of something like this," he said. "Where did you go? I couldn't find you."

She told him about the dream as he held her close, comforting her.

"You have seen the ghost-soul of my mother, Odakai," said Vaylance, "but what it means, I do not know."

He lifted and carried her into the bedroom, and, setting her gently on the bed, he lay down beside her.

She had avoided any affectionate gestures from him all day, being both attracted and repelled by his vampire nature. But now, partly because she was upset, and partly because he would be leaving soon, she pressed closer in his arms.

"If you yield to me now," he said, "I will make your blood to sing."

She could feel his breath on her neck and she braced herself for what she knew must come next. But he didn't bite. He kissed her tenderly, and then he was kissing her mouth and her nose and her eyes and carefully undressing her. "Why you're tattooed!" she said, when he took off his shirt.

She traced with her finger where a stag raced across his chest.

"It's my soul-beast," he told her.

They played at love for a long time. He was gentle, teasing, the most sensitive lover she had ever known.

◆ ◆ ◆

Vaylance, when he saw the soft fur of her bosom, made a little cry of joy. This and her scent proved to him that she was one of his own kind, and he banished his Christian conscience to a remote corner of his mind where it could not touch him.

When he finally pulled her over on top of him and entered her, she was so close that she could hardly contain it, but he sensed this and stopped, then brought her close to the knife's edge several times before allowing her to finish. And her blood sang, pulsing in her ears, a song of the open steppes. As she lay satiated on top of him, he sought the jugular vein in her throat and bit deeply. She didn't really mind. She felt so warm and sleepy that she was content to lie there and enjoy the intimacy of it. When he finished, he licked the wound clean with his pink dog-like tongue, and Myrna, having recovered, reached up and nipped him playfully in the throat.

"My poor little wolf with no teeth," he said. "I must help you." And he turned his head and bit his own shoulder so that the blood flowed.

"I share myself with you," he said.

She looked at the red trickle. She knew what he wanted her to do, but she didn't want to do it. So she just stared down at him.

"You reject me then?" he asked with such soft, wounded eyes that she couldn't refuse him. She pressed her lips to the small cut and drank a little of the warm liquid. The taste of his blood awoke in her some ancient need and she continued to drink until it was satisfied. For an instant it seemed as if she saw herself through his eyes. The moment passed and she was aware that he looked at her intently.

"Our souls have touched," he said.

They lay together a long time without talking.

Vaylance's conscience uncoiled from where it lay sleeping like a dormant asp and bit him.

"I have sinned and must repent," he said. "The Christians have such strange rules about love."

Then he looked at her and brushed back her hair to kiss her forehead. "And yet I don't think God would begrudge me to share blood-love with you," he said, "because it's such a comfort, and doesn't the Bible say, 'Comfort ye, comfort ye, my people, saith the Lord'?"

Myrna laughed.

"Have I made a joke?" he asked.

"Sort of," she said. "That's the first time I ever heard anyone quote the Bible to justify fornication."

Hurt, he rolled away from her, pulling the pillow down over his head.

"You make it sound like something people write on the wall of a latrine," he said.

Myrna pulled the pillow away and was going to clout him with it, when she saw that although his eyes were tightly closed, a tear wet the lashes.

"Hey, I'm sorry," she said. "I was only teasing you."

"It's nothing," he said. "Just my romantic nature showing. I'd hoped we could call it love, not fornication. But I know it's much too soon to know."

He was silent for a moment and then he said, "Do you know why it's so difficult for you to love, Myrna?"

"No," she said honestly, almost guiltily. "I thought it was because I'd been hurt once, but I know it goes much deeper than that."

"It's because the wolvish soul builds trust slowly," he said. "It rejects all but those who persistently continue to take the risk of courting it. It may be befriended, never tamed."

Myrna felt that, for the first time, someone had really understood her nature. It seemed impossible that he could be leaving.

"I wish we had more time," she said.

"So do I," he said, "but perhaps we may meet again someday. I think that dream you had gives us cause for hope. It may mean that Odakai accepts you, but you are just not ready yet."

They held each other for a long time in the dark, saying nothing.

From somewhere in the room, Myrna seemed to hear a faraway voice, singing in an unknown language, his language.

"I must leave you now," he said.

"I wish I could go with you," she said, "but if wishes were horses, then beggars would ride."

He didn't understand the English proverb, and she had to explain to him that back in the 17th century only those with enough money could afford a horse.

"It sounds funny to me," he said, "because where I come from even the beggars ride. I'll change the saying around and give you my blessing as a parting gift. May your wishes be horses, Myrna, and carry you wherever you desire to go."

"May your wishes be horses," she said. "I like the sound of that."

He gave her a parting kiss and an affectionate little nip on the neck, and then he was gone.

## IV

In 1845 it was raining. Vaylance slogged back toward camp in the evening drizzle. On the way to the medical tent, he passed the cook's station. Old, fat Temboyov was boiling a vat of some kind of lumpy gray porridge and bragging to a new recruit about how he'd looted a set of porcelain tea cups. Vaylance surreptitiously relieved him of a few of the saucers.

The crossmatch worked just as she said it would. He was able to rule out any incompatible donors by watching for red clumps against the white porcelain background. The transfusion was a success, and Dr. Rimsky was up and around on the third day. Vaylance moved back into the medical tent, after spending two days sleeping in a hollow tree.

"I'm relieved to see that you are not slinking into camp looking like a drowned rat anymore," said Rimsky. "But why didn't you just take your bed and claim illness? I would have thought up some way to cover for you."

"Because no one would believe me," said Vaylance. "I look healthier than the lot of you."

It was true. His complexion was almost rosy. Thanks to the transfusion in Myrna's hospital, Vaylance was in better health than he'd been in a long time.

"What's that tune you keep humming?" asked Dr. Rimsky one night as they worked together in the tent.

"I think it's called 'The Waters of Time,' " answered Vaylance, a little sadly.

## V

Externally, Myrna's life did not change much after Vaylance left. Work was still a series of frantic rush orders interspersed with periods of boredom. She brought a book on Russian history to the hospital to read when she wasn't needed.

Shanty still moved his big feet with the grace of a fairy dancer, and she won another blue ribbon at the shows. But he could not carry her to the place she really desired to go. One Saturday afternoon as she brushed the saddle marks out of his hair, she pressed her face into his neck and wet his mane with tears. It was then that she heard him make the little noise in the throat, as horses do when they wish to express sympathy, and she realized she had allowed herself to love again.

That night when she went to sleep, she dreamed that she walked through a long, dark tunnel. She came out into a large grassy place under a starry night sky. A horse and rider approached, making no sound except the jingling of faint harness bells. As the figure drew closer, Myrna recognized the Cossack woman who carried the wolf cub. The dark-eyed woman stopped her horse and offered the cub to Myrna, who took it and held it close to her heart. The woman pointed to a rutted wagon road, then turned her horse and rode away making no noise of hooves but only the ringing of tiny bells.

Myrna followed the road indicated until she came to a wagon parked by the roadside. A man was just climbing up to the driver's seat. Myrna put the cub on the wagon bed and boosted herself up. There were men, some lying, some sitting up, in the wagon. The man nearest her was crudely bandaged about the head and he muttered softly to himself. The driver clucked to the horses and the wagon creaked on its way. Myrna tucked the small wolf under the light flannel she was wearing. She felt its cold nose against her bare breasts. It was getting colder, so she moved closer to the man and placed her back against the side of the wagon. They lurched along until the road turned in at a large tent. Horses were tethered in a small grove of oak trees, and there was a fire a little ways from the tent. The driver pulled up and said something in Russian. A sturdy, gray-haired man with a bandaged arm came out of the tent and spoke to the driver, who climbed down from his seat.

Myrna reached for the wolf cub and found it was missing. She looked down the front of her flannel gown and saw that in the hollow between her breasts, her little patch of gray fur was denser. Before she had time to think about this, she heard a voice she recognized from inside the tent. She jumped down from the wagon, and, ignoring the gray-haired man who spoke to her, ducked under the flap and entered.

Inside, in the lantern light, she saw him, with his back toward her, bending over a patient. He turned to look her way and his mouth fell open in astonishment so that his blood teeth showed.

"Myrna!" he cried, and stepping around a cot, he hugged her to his white, blood-stained apron, then held her back to look at her.

"Like all dreamwalkers, you have come ill-prepared," he said, plucking at her flannel night gown. "And barefoot too."

She looked down past her ruffled hem to where her bare toes peeked out. He rummaged in a corner of the tent and tossed her a wool shirt, a pair of trousers and two heavy-knit woolen socks.

"This will have to do for now," he said. "We have incoming wounded and I have work to do." He was already busy with scissors, cutting back the sleeve of a soldier's uniform.

Myrna saw his surgical tools—forceps, scalpels, needles—all lying in neat order on a dirty piece of linen.

"You could stand to learn a few things about asepsis," she said, and made a mental note that she would have to teach him sterile technique. She hunted until she found a pot and water to boil, and took it out to put on the fire. Then she returned to where Vaylance bent over his patient, speaking soothing Russian phrases, as he pried at a musket ball in the ragged flesh. She found the bandaging cloth and made ready to assist him.

# SMALL CHANGES

SPAREEN THE VARKELA leechman cleaned his scalpel in the boiling water and moved away from the fire toward the thick felt wall of the nomad yurt, where his patient lay wrapped in a sheepskin blanket. Around the fire pit the Nogai Tartars squatted, watching suspiciously, one of them smoking tobacco in a small silver pipe. Cold, gray evening rain pelted the yurt, sometimes entering the smoke hole in the roof to hiss in the fire pit.

Spareen motioned to the Tartars.

"If two of you hold him, I'll dig that musket ball out of his leg now."

He peeled back the sheepskin, raised the hem of the man's robe and two of the Tartars, with small mutterings, came and held their comrade as Spareen began to probe

133

cautiously in the wound. The bleeding burst forth again, bright arterial blood, as Spareen's scalpel ticked against something hard. With a quick movement of his wrist, he flicked the bit of lead onto the Turkish carpet and applied pressure to the wound. The cloth rapidly darkened with fresh blood, and Spareen's needle-thin, hollow blood-teeth slipped involuntarily out of the small niches in his upper jaw. One of the Nogais gasped and pointed at the exposed were-teeth.

"You needn't worry," said Spareen. "Varkela never take blood from a sick person. If I save his life, I'll take some blood from one of his relatives later in payment. I don't know what superstitions you've heard about my people, but be assured I am not a walking dead or Vampire."

This near the Russian settlements, some Tartars had forgotten the ways of the Varkela, known as bringers of healing to their ancestors. And well they might forget, for his people were a rarity this far west of the Volga.

The flow of blood seemed to abate. Spareen pulled back the cloth and observed that clotting had begun to take place. He bent low over the wound and gave the area a quick swipe with his pink, doglike tongue. The last seepage stopped. A good trick that, thought Spareen, noting the amazed look from the Nogais. He deftly bandaged the area and returned to the fire. Now, if the fellow had not lost too much blood, he would recover and Spareen would earn his much-needed payment. His veins ached hollowly for the *blood-price*, as the showing teeth had betrayed.

"If it's not too much trouble, I could do with a bit to eat," said Spareen, hoping to quell one hunger by feeding another. He knew that it was often good practice to fill one's belly in the presence of outbloods. It seemed to affirm a common bond and make him seem less mysterious to humankind.

After a bit of bustling about in the stewpot they offered him meat cooked with buckwheat groats and gravy—horsemeat! His gorge rose in his throat at this horror, until he realized that they in truth did not intend it as an insult, but were probably unacquainted with the ways of the Varkela, and reduced to such straits by their poverty. He declined their hospitality, choosing his words carefully so as not to offend:

"Just as you who are followers of the prophet abstain from pork, so I am constrained by my religion against eating the flesh of the horse." Religion was not the exact reason, but it sounded convincing.

He bid them good evening and passed out the leather door flap of the yurt, hearing them answer, "Many smiles," as was their custom.

The golden-eyes mare was waiting for him, calmly pulling at cottony milfoil that grew in profusion by the yurt. From his saddlebags he offered her a handful of corn, which she eagerly gobbled up.

"Not too much now. You'll get colic," he warned.

"Me overindulge?" she snorted, in the horse language that only the Varkela understand. "That's your vice, not mine."

She tried to catch in her teeth the wine flask that hung from his belt, but he was too quick for her, snaring her head in the bridle so that all she got was cold steel between her teeth.

"You're a nuisance," he said, hiding the disputed wine flask in a saddlebag. "You can't stand the idea that somebody might be having a good time."

"What I can't stand is carrying your inebriated carcass home in the morning," said the mare. "What if a wolf should come along? I rely on the fellow in the saddle to haul out his flintlock and protect me."

"If a wolf did come along, and I were as drunk as you

always imply, he'd smell my breath and faint," Spareen chuckled, tightening the girth.

The golden-eyes mare heaved a heavy horse sigh as he slung his pharmacopoeia of herbs over the saddle and vaulted into place on her back.

"If you can't make a large change in your behavior, you might consider at least making a small one," she suggested, as she set out through the tall grass of the steppe for his next patient.

"Either drink less, or drink something less potent," she advised.

"I'll give the matter due consideration," said Spareen.

◆ ◆ ◆

As they slogged along a wagon track, the rain increased, pouring a deluge over the steppe, making a creek of the road. Water rolled down Spareen's thick wool burka to soak his white doeskin trousers at the knee. What a miserable night to be out making his rounds. Better the pothouse in one of the sleepy little Cossack villages along the Terek. There he might buy a taste of something stronger than wine to ease the hunger of his were-teeth, might even snare a wench to warm his belly-fur, if he felt so inclined, and if he could convince his nose to accept the stench of an outblood woman. Any excuse would do to get out of this never-ending downpour.

It was then that he saw six white, bubble-shaped mounds poking up from the steppe like puffball mushrooms, the yurts of Kalmuck Tartars. This would be as good a place as any to wait out the rain. And perhaps he could drum up a few patients.

Spareen urged the mare off the wagon road into the high feather grass, which painted wetness on the cuffs of his doeskin britches. He reined in at one of the dwellings and called out the traditional greeting of his people:

"Does anyone here require healing?"

An orange gap opened in the night as a felt flap was pulled back. Black shapes, silhouetted by a triangle of fire, observed him.

"Welcome, stranger," one of them called.

Spareen dismounted and ducked his large body through the opening.

"I am Zebek," a flat-faced, snub-nosed Kalmuck addressed him. The fellow wore a pillbox hat from which a queue hung down the back, and was dressed in a dark-blue, padded jacket, with frog-buttons, that hung to his knees. Under this he wore the baggy trousers of a house-man of the steppe. Kalmucks!—what a bit of luck to stumble on one of their settlements. They were usually found farther east, and Spareen's father had had his practice among these hardy folk in his keep beyond the Volga. Nogais out here had forgotten much, but Kalmucks had migrated in a much more recent wave, and would therefore know what manner of beast a Varkela was.

Spareen settled to the thick felt floor of the yurt and began to shed his wet clothes in layers.

"If I might sleep here a while, I can repay you. My camp is somewhat distant, and I am wet to the bone." He pulled the furry shapka from his head and rung out the water to show the truth of his word.

"No need for payment," said Zebek. "It is our custom to take in the sojourner and the stranger within our gates."

An odd speech for a Kalmuck, thought Spareen, and he was briefly reminded of the quaint-sounding phrases of a Nogai Tartar quoting Koran. But the Kalmucks were Buddhist of the Tibetan school, and perhaps this was one of their sayings, although he'd never heard it before.

Zebek, who looked to be about forty, moved some bedding toward Spareen to make a place for him to stretch out. Two children, a boy and a girl, huddled close by the fire, and a young girl in her teens, apparently the eldest daughter, sat cross-legged, sewing while the mother leaned over the fire, stirring something in the kettle.

Spareen shucked off his white doeskin shirt and scratched at his fur-covered belly. This seemed to fascinate the teenaged girl who stared at him with slant eyes almost round in curiosity. She put out a hand as if to touch, but her father stopped her with a curt word. Probably never saw a Varkela without his shirt before, thought Spareen, gratefully covering himself with a dry blanket. He pulled out his wine flask and offered it to his host, who sat on his haunches observing Spareen through slitted eyes.

The Kalmuck sniffed at the flask and then placed it to his lips and upended it, taking a long pull. He handed it back to Spareen, who drained it and then held it upside down over the fire to show it was empty. The lord of the domicile reached for a bottle that hung from the pole frame of the yurt, containing a clear fluid that Spareen at first thought was water, until Zebek uncorked it and Spareen smelled arrack, a potent brandy distilled from fermented mare's milk. They passed this bottle back and forth for a long while—it was throat-burning stuff but it cheered the belly, and soon Spareen was feeling warm and sleepy. He wasn't sure of the exact moment that he drifted off—he had a vague recollection of someone pulling a blanket over him—and then he slowed his heart and breathing and settled into the deathlike state that passes for sleep among the Varkela.

He awoke to find himself on his back lying in the tall grass a little ways away from the yurt. The sun was sitting like a bright orange ball on the western edge of the steppe. Great bloods and butterflies! He'd slept the whole day, and it was again time for him to begin a night's work. He sat up and saw Zebek's eldest daughter coming toward him carrying mare's milk in a soft leather sack. When she saw him she dropped the bucket and screamed. Spareen cast his eyes about the ground expecting to see a snake but found none. When he looked again, he saw the stout figure of the mother brandishing the cast-iron cook pot. This descended on his head with a resounding crack and he faded again from consciousness.

When he next opened his eyes, he found himself securely tied, with sturdy ropes cutting into his wrists and ankles. His head throbbed painfully. By the stars Spareen judged it to be about eight o'clock in the evening, if he had not lost another day. Zebek was squatting nearby, engaged in stretching a sheep hide on a frame. He looked up suddenly, apparently drawn by Spareen's stirring, reached into his shirt and pulled out a talisman on the end of a string and held it toward Spareen, saying:

"Be still, demon!"

The talisman twinkled in the light from the fire that shone through the door flap—and it was then that Spareen recognized the cause and the seriousness of his situation. A cross with a slanted crosspiece at the bottom—a Russian crucifix—dangled at the end of the string.

Spareen shrank back from it as far as his bonds would let him, for in his religion this was "the sun's hammer," an unlucky sign similar to the "evil eye." He averted his eyes from it as much as possible, for to look at it would increase his bad luck—not that it could get much worse, he thought. These Kalmucks were apparently converts to the Russian Orthodox religion, having little knowledge of their former relationship to the Varkela, and having fallen heir to the usual Christian prejudice against the *Children of the Night*.

Zebek's stout wife poked her head out of the door flap, the firelight gleaming on her oily features.

"The corpse wakes again," Zebek informed her, and Spareen realized they were speaking of him.

"I was not dead, only sleeping," he said. "I am a Varkela leechman, not a corpse. Our sleep is different from yours. If you have any illness among your horses, your sheep or yourselves, I shall try to cure it free of charge to prove to you my benign nature." He was careful not to mention what his fee would have been.

"We will let the priest decide what manner of creature you are. He visits this encampment once a week to hold service," said Zebek. His knuckles whitened as he tightened the tanning frame.

"And when will that be?" asked Spareen.

"In four days." Zebek propped the taut frame against the side of the yurt.

"You might offer me something to eat," said Spareen. "It's been two days since I last filled my belly."

"Does a demon eat?" asked the wife.

"I don't know about demons," said Spareen, "but I am Varkela, and we most certainly do eat."

Zebek's wife stared at him doubtfully, then went back inside. She returned with a helping of lamb on a wooden plate. With a large serving ladle she offered him over-large, steaming mouthfuls, which he licked up as best he could, burning his wolvish tongue, but not complaining for fear she might stop.

The plate was soon empty, but Spareen, being a big fellow, probably outweighing both Zebek and his wife, voiced a hope for more, and received it in great measure. At least they didn't intend to starve him. Madam Zebek seemed to enjoy stuffing him and he obliged her, gobbling happily and polishing the plate with his tongue when she presented it for him to lick. On a full stomach the nature of his plight did not seem so dire. He would merely wait until they had all gone to sleep and call the golden-eyes mare to help him escape. But where had she gotten to?

He passed his eyes over the scruffy steppe ponies of Zebek's herd—a scrawny, ill-fed bunch as he had ever seen—until he spied her sleek buckskin profile, and called to her softly in the old language. She merely looked at him sadly and raised her left rear hoof to show that it was chained to a heavy stake. Her golden eyes reproached him, saying, "This is all your fault." And well he knew it! How foolish to allow himself to be captured by the cross-worshippers. He had never been so careless among the Cossacks, knowing full well the fate of suspected "Vampires," but he had never before encountered Christian converts among the Tartars. This could be a bad business indeed.

Still, he had his wits about him, and apparently four days until the priest was due. Perhaps he could play with their demon beliefs to his advantage.

"How do you intend to keep me here?" he inquired. "For if you sleep, I will make a spirit knife to set me free."

"Then we will post a guard," said Zebek, falling for Spareen's ruse. A single guard, hopefully.

"No, please don't do that!" wailed Spareen. "And especially don't let me be guarded by a woman, else I'll never leave this place."

"Thank you for telling me this, foolish demon," said Zebek. "This night my wife and daughter will guard you in shifts."

Spareen moaned and groaned and tried to sound appropriately miserable, while inwardly rejoicing that Zebek was so gullible.

They built a watch fire outside the yurt, and some of Zebek's neighbors came to stare and poke at the "demon." One, an elderly, stoop-shouldered graybeard named Shambai–Noyon, stopped and peered through crusted lids at Spareen. Another avenue of hope opened in Spareen's mind.

"Truly, Father, I am not really a demon but a member

of the race called Varkela—surely you have lived long
enough to have heard of my people. We are healers."

"Varkela ..." muttered the elder. "An odd name.
Where have I heard it before?"

"You have a scar on your nose," said Spareen. "Perhaps as a child, your father brought you to be protected
against smallpox, by a Varkela leechman." Spareen re-
ferred to the Oriental method of vaccination in which
infected material was placed in the nose.

"Yes ... there was something like that ... I don't
remember well. Too many of my memories are clouded
with age—like mare's milk too long fermented, the whey
is bitter. Most people were lost in the 'Great Migration.'
I don't like to think of those times." He was referring to
the migration of Kalmucks in 1777, when a large party
of them tried to return to Mongolia. Most of them died
in the harsh Siberian winter.

"I am sorry, elder," said Spareen. "I did not mean to
cause you pain. But if you remember Varkela, let me try
to heal your eyes to prove that I am what I say. Do not
let them turn me over to the Russian priest who will cut
out my heart and burn it."

"Too many memories," said the elder. "I must go and
settle them with sleep." And Spareen's hope in that direction slipped away.

The first guard posted was Zebek's teenaged daughter,
Neshe. She sat at the fire, at as far a distance from him
as possible, and sewed with demurely lowered eyes, her
fingers plucking the needle back and forth as she plunged
it through the thick cloth.

"What are you making?" asked Spareen, hoping to engage her eyes.

"Trousers," she said, not looking at him. The needle
flickered in the firelight.

"For whom?" he asked.

"For myself." She continued to concentrate on her sewing, her small fingers working swiftly.

"You're a very pretty girl, do you know that?"

"You're a demon. How would you know?"

"Look me in the eye, and I'll tell you how I know."

She raised her head and looked straight at him with eyes full of trusting innocence. Ah, she had never heard the rumors about the ways of Varkela with women. It was almost too easy to witch her with his dark Varkela eyes, making her desire him, luring her to come and kneel before him, awaiting his pleasure. Carefully, he hunched forward, trying to catch the handle of the little kinjal she wore at her waist in his teeth. He hoped it was a real knife with a sharpened blade, not just a womanish decoration. Patiently, she knelt there, an unmoving automaton, while he pushed at her with his head, trying to snare the small dagger's handle with lips or teeth. There! He had it!

"Neshe! Pull back!" came a cry from the doorway of the yurt. Immediately the girl came to her senses and gave Spareen a good smack with her forearm that sent him sprawling.

"You didn't really think I'd trust the sayings of a demon, did you?" said Zebek, stepping forth from the yurt, his dark, oiled features shining in the fire's glare. "You have some power over women, but I outsmarted you. Now we'll see how you manage with two strong men to guard you. Zagan! Come watch with me," he called to one of the other six dwellings, and another Kalmuck appeared carrying an old-fashioned matchlock weapon.

Spareen's spirits sank. A woman he could witch, and single man he might possibly have mesmerized, but two of them insured that there would be no chance of escaping this night. To comfort himself he raised his mighty voice and sang a song in the Varkela tongue about the wolf-minded girls of his own people, how they could not be witched, and how much he desired to marry with one. This just made him sadder, for Varkela women were few, due to an illness that claimed many of them before puberty, and there was little chance he would ever marry. When dawn came, two more of them arrived to guard him, and he rolled over, pressing his face into the sweet grasses to block out the cruel light of day, and slept his death-sleep again.

His people, the Varkela, had originated, according to their tradition, in the Altai Mountain region north of Mongolia. Since time immemorial they had plied their healing trade among the nomads of the steppe. In A.D. 400 many of them had migrated west with the hordes of Attila the Hun, who welcomed these practitioners of leechcraft to bind up the wounds of many battles. They were an old race and were dying out, but occasionally here or there one might run across one of these strange fellows who spoke the horse's language, slept during the daylight hours, healed the sick and, as the price of healing, drew a cupful of blood through thin, hollow were-teeth. Their reputation as healers was outstanding, as it had to be—for one had to produce cures to earn payment in human blood. And so Spareen had followed his calling, gelding colts, worming sheep, pulling teeth, cooling fevers, to earn his necessary fee, as his fathers had done for centuries before him. But hard times had brought him to these more western territories where his people were a memory that had perhaps lent substance to the Vampire myth.

When he next awoke, his blood-teeth ached like twin mounds in his upper jaw, and he knew he would have to feed their hunger soon, but his first concern was to gain his freedom from this captivity. The pale light of dusk greeted his eyes when he opened them and above him, Shambai–Noyon, the aged one, looked down at him, a gray pigtail swinging free over one shoulder.

"Tell me, young man, if you are not a demon, why do you cringe at the sign of the cross?" he asked Spareen.

"Because I am Varkela," said Spareen. "In my religion, the cross is not the symbol of your teacher, Christ, but rather a sign representing the 'hammer of the sun.' The name 'Varkela' means *Children of the Night*, and we worship Our Lady Moon, so the sun is the devil and we shun his sight. That is why we sometimes say of the Christians, 'Their god is our devil.'"

"Well answered," said Shambai, running a hand through his sparse gray beard. "There is truth in you, in spite of your attempt to deceive Zebek and his daughter. In fact, as I recall, your kind has a nefarious reputation with regard to women—but let us put you to the test. We have decided to give you a chance. If you are truly Varkela, then, as my father taught me, you can cure any disease, and we have a patient on whom you can prove yourself."

"I can't heal all diseases," said Spareen, "but I will most certainly try."

"We have agreed that if you can heal this person, you will go free, but if not, we will save you for the priest to examine. If you are Varkela, as you say, you should have no trouble proving it."

Spareen wanted to protest that he was not some sort of wizard, but decided it would be of no use. It was ironic to be in a situation where for once the reports about his race were too glowing to live up to, rather than the usual malign rumors he'd heard out in this territory.

"I am going to untie your hands and bring you your things," said Shambai. "But I'm warning you not to try to escape. Zebek mistrusts you for trying to trick him. I have some say over him, being an elder of the council, but he says he'll put a bullet into you if you make a wrong move, and there's little I could do to stop him, but he's agreed to abide by the results of the test."

"And what will be the test?" asked Spareen uneasily. He hoped it was some curable illness, not healing of a hopeless cripple as their teacher, Christ, was reported to have done.

"I will bring you the patient, my young grandson, Yulay."

They brought the boy, who looked fairly healthy. Spareen was glad that he was not a cripple, and that it was not a life-or-death matter, but his heart despaired when they removed the child's shirt to reveal an angry papular rash over most of his back and chest. There are millions of things that can cause such a rash, thought Spareen, and he doubted that he'd be able to find a cure in three short days, but he knew he must try. If a Christian priest took a close look inside his mouth, it would all be over.

Patiently he began to question them about the rash. When had it appeared? How long had it lasted? Was there fever?

He wasn't able to ascertain too much. The boy had had the rash chronically off and on for about four years, which ruled out contagious, short-term diseases like measles, smallpox, sheep pox and scarlet fever. The child seemed to have it more in the winter than in the summer, and usually just on his upper body, but on rare occasions, on his legs and thighs also.

Spareen racked his brain trying to think of a source of the symptoms. The rash was apparently seasonal—could it be an effect of cold weather, perhaps? There were many conditions that were seasonal. He was reminded of his brother Vaylance's seasonal asthma attacks, brought on by exposure to certain flowers in the springtime. He had an idea!

"Bring me all the boy's clothes and let me cut a small patch from each garment." Spareen set out to test his theory, praising Mircafta, the lady in the moon, for giving him this burst of insight. It was only one chance out of hundreds that he'd be right, but it was the only thing he'd thought of that had a cure close to hand.

"Keep the child inside near the fire, and do not let him wear anything on the upper part of his body."

Two days later all the people of the settlement came to see the results of Spareen's test.

"You see," said Spareen, "there is no rash around the patch of flax or the one of linen that represents his summer clothes." He pointed to the patches of cloth that he had fixed to the boy's thigh with drops of warm tallow. "And you can see that his rash has cleared up after two days without a shirt. This patch of rabbit fur also shows no rash but look at this one. . . ." He pointed to the patch of wool. Around it the skin had reddened and it must have itched for the child kept trying to scratch.

"You see, his skin is sensitive to wool which he wears in winter, or on cold days. In the summer he wears flax, linen, or no shirt at all, and he doesn't suffer. But in the winter, the wool itches and he scratched the irritation, making it worse, until a rash forms. Fortunately, a small change in behavior will solve the problem. Make him a winter shirt of rabbit pelts, and he should have no more cause to scratch.

"He's proved himself Varkela," said Shambai–Noyon. "As my father said, they can cure all diseases."

"Not all diseases," said Spareen. "But I believe I have an ointment in my pouch that will do for those crusty eyelids of yours."

"And now about the matter of payment," said the aged Kalmuck.

"My freedom is payment enough," said Spareen, not wishing to arouse any more superstitious thoughts among them by revealing his need for blood.

"No, you deserve other payment," Shambai insisted. "My little grandson suffered four years until you came along." Then he said, lowering his voice that only Spareen might hear, "Let me have the honor of paying the *blood-price* for my clan. I am a gray-haired elder of the council, and you must respect my wishes."

"Well, since you put it that way, how can I refuse," said Spareen. "But let us go into your yurt, away from prying eyes that might misunderstand."

In the darkness of Shambai–Noyon's dwelling, after applying a leather thong as a tourniquet, Spareen slipped one needle-thin tooth into the proper vein of the old man's proffered forearm, and drank a scant cupful of the red juice of life into his blood-starved vessels, enough to keep his hunger quiet for a time.

And before Spareen could take his leave, the old Tartar pressed a gift into his hand, which Spareen tried half-heartedly to refuse, but at last gave in without too much persuading.

"It wasn't much of a cure," he told the golden-eyes mare while saddling her. "But at least I earned my freedom." He pulled tight the cinch and climbed aboard.

"And now I suppose you'll swill all your wine to celebrate, if I know you," said the mare.

"No wine tonight; I've changed my ways," said Spareen. "I've decided to take your advice and make a small change in my behavior."

The ears of the golden-eyes mare stood straight up like musket bayonets. She swung her head around and stared at him, saying:

"I've been hoping to hear you say that for a long time."

Spareen grinned down at her, a bottle of Muscovite vodka, the old Kalmuck's gift, clenched in his ham-sized fist.

"I might have known!" shrilled the mare. She set out for the wagon road at a bone-shaking trot. "I suppose you think that's doing better," she neighed angrily, kicking up small rocks in her path.

Above them gray clouds scudded across the moon,

threatening rain again, but in spite of that, Spareen felt it would be a beautiful night for singing. As they made their way along the wagon track between windswept oceans of waving feather grass, a plover broke cover, keening as it mounted, flapping into the wind.

"Some people don't know an improvement when they see one," sighed Spareen, slipping the vodka flask back into his pocket.

# SPAREEN AND OLD TURK

SPAREEN THE VARKELA leechman sat in his yurt smoking tobacco with Iskendar Khan one summer's evening. Iskendar Khan's proud Circassian nose threw a hawk's beak shadow on the gray felt wall. He was a wiry little man, a Cherkess from the Caucasus, who had moved to the steppe to avoid a blood feud, adopted a nomadic life, and taken to breeding horses in his old age.

"I can help you win that woman of yours, Spareen," he said, drawing deep on his pipe and allowing the smoke to return through his nose. "If you will capture for me Old Turk, my people will take you on as leechman. You will earn rivers of blood for yourself and your bride."

It was a tempting proposition, thought Spareen, the tips of his were-teeth poking hungrily into his lower lip.

His blood thirsting Varkura would certainly like the end result, even if she did not care for the means.

"You must give me time to think it over," he finally said.

Spareen pondered this carefully in his heart for the next few days. Old Turk was almost a legend on the steppe, an exceptional stallion that some claimed had escaped when the Turkish sultan sent some horses as a gift to the Czar. Whatever his origin, Old Turk was a magnificent horse of the Arab–Turkmen type, and his offspring invariably inherited the endurance and speed which made him impossible to capture. Sometimes on a clear, moonless night, Spareen, returning from his night's rounds, had seen the old fellow, drifting like a gray ghost above the silvery bear-grass. Sometimes Spareen had called to him in the horse language, but the only answer he received was "No time to visit. I want to run." And with a flash of his silvery tail, Old Turk was gone to roam the steppe and bless the mares of rich and poor alike with bounty of his seed. For what greater joy to the poor steppes nomad after a harsh Russian winter than a few sturdy foals capable of bringing a good price at the yearling market in Astrakhan.

"It's an evil deed, Spareen," said the golden-eyes mare when Spareen went to talk it over with her. "You mustn't do it."

"I agree, it's an evil deed," said Spareen. "But I am unemployed and weary of the quest. Summer is almost over and winter will be on us soon. If I take the khan's offer, I will have enough for myself and Varkura, and if I do not, it will be a hard winter living from vein to vein, feeding only when people are desperate and sick enough to seek me out. I must do it, evil as it may seem."

"If you do this thing, I shall not speak to you," said the golden-eyes mare.

"Very well," said Spareen. "You never say much that's useful anyhow."

The golden-eyes mare said nothing and seemed to take a sudden interest in a patch of dragon's tooth, tugging briskly with her teeth.

"I will do it," he told the khan the next evening. But his conscience bothered him, for as a Varkela he respected the free, wild stallion of the steppe.

Fighting his better nature, Spareen strode out into the night and began to sing in horse language. He passed a tamarisk hillock and sat down with his back to it. Soon he was rewarded with a clatter of hooves, and the great gray horse, his tail streaming like a banner, came to him. The Old Turk stopped a few inches from Spareen and nosed his chamois-leather shirt.

"What do you want with me?" asked the stallion.

"I would ask a favor of you," said Spareen, and he began to explain his troubles to the Turk. "If you would only allow me to capture you for Iskendar Khan and agree to cover his mares, I would be able to support myself and my woman."

"A pretty proposition for you," said the stallion, "but what about me? Covering mares is all right in its way, but for me to live is to run free."

"Then you won't cooperate?"

"That sharp-fanged woman has turned your head, Spareen. If you were in your right mind you would not ask this of me." And with a switch of his silvery tail, he galloped off into the night.

"You leave me no choice, then," Spareen called, "but to run you down.

◆ ◆ ◆

The next night Spareen set off with a string of several horses, the best runners in his herd. Finding Old Turk's favorite territory, Spareen staked these horses at five-mile intervals and left them standing: saddled, bridled, and ready to ride. By dawn he was ready to begin his search. The golden-eyes mare cantered along the crest of a small hill while Spareen scanned the plain below for any sign of his quarry. The eastern edge of the steppe paled to gold as the sun rose. Spareen took his black eye-cloth out and tied it over his eyes. Then he and the mare descended the hill to the steppe below. It was a fresh morning. Dew glittered on the grasses and the bittersweet smell of sage filled the air.

They rode in a wide circle around the perimeter of the Turk's territory and gradually closed in. By midday they had circumscribed the territory twice without spotting the stallion. Still, the perimeter was many miles long. A horse could hide behind a tamarisk hillock and not be seen.

Spareen dismounted and poured himself a bowl of koumiss from his leathern bag. The warm, sour milk went down easily, and he lay on his back for a while to watch a hawk drifting overhead. Where could the Turk be hiding? Perhaps he was not in his usual range but had moved eastward toward the Caspian.

"Don't you smell his scent on the wind?" he asked the golden-eyes mare. "I was sure I did."

The golden-eyes mare said nothing.

"All right, be that way, then," said Spareen and climbed back into the saddle.

They travelled until the late-afternoon sun was glinting off the distant Caucasus. They had just topped a familiar ridge when Spareen heard a great scrambling of hooves, and Old Turk rolled to his feet from where he'd been caught napping in the tall grasses.

Spareen swore. "He was right under my nose the whole time! I could have passed within one-fourth of a verst and never seen him. No wonder my nose smelled him." In that grassy country a bit of gray on the ground

could easily be taken for a stone. Spareen called to the
stallion, but received no answer. He urged the golden-
eyes mare to follow at a discreet distance, always pressing
the stallion toward the east where a fresh horse waited.

They covered five miles that way, until Spareen
bounced down from the mare, caught the reins of his
next horse and continued the chase. He marveled that
the big gray's pace did not slacken as the day wore on
into night. Spareen changed mounts three times, and he
was still no nearer his quarry.

He knew the gray would have to stop for water soon.
His own horse was becoming winded and would also
welcome a drink from one of the creeks that flowed into
the Terek. Perhaps if the Turk stopped to drink, he
would become water-bellied and not able to outpace
Spareen's horse.

The moon rose over the steppe, bathing the sage in
blue milky light. Old Turk slowed as he came to one of
the creeks. Spareen reined in and held back to give the
gray a chance to drink his fill. But the Turk merely
stopped for an instant to take a few swallows and was
then off again, quick as ever, eluding Spareen's noose
with easy grace.

Two mounts later, in the gray dawn, Spareen admitted
defeat and turned back toward camp with his winded
horses. In a way he was glad that he had failed. It was
a crime to trap such beauty.

◆ ◆ ◆

When he told Iskendar Khan of his results, the khan
was not pleased. Rubbing his hawk's beak, he said:

"Since you are unable, Spareen, perhaps I must hire
a good shot to crease that stallion's neck and stun him
until we can get a rope on him."

Spareen was appalled. He would never consider creasing a horse, for the margin for error was very narrow. A few inches lower would not merely stun but kill a horse.

"You would risk killing the Turk in order to capture him?" asked Spareen. He didn't like the fire that burned in Iskendar Khan's eyes.

"I must bring Old Turk in to settle my mares—a better breed of horse—that will be my legacy to my sons!" declared the khan. His wealth was in fat-tailed sheep, but his chief love was his brood of sturdy Turkmen mares carefully selected for their conformation. Spareen could not deny that they were all proud examples of the old Turkmen stock, and he could not blame Iskendar Khan for wanting to breed them to a superior stallion of their own kind. Still he tried to dissuade him.

"You could improve your stock by breeding to the Kabardin stud in the Caucasus," he ventured.

Iskendar Khan made an impatient gesture.

"You know that's not the same," he said.

"Before you damage that worthy horse, give me one more chance at catching him," said Spareen. "I have an idea."

◆ ◆ ◆

As Spareen left the khan his conscience troubled him. He realized that the last thing he desired was seeing Old Turk a captive in the khan's stud. Still, he couldn't bear the thought that someone might crease the Turk and miss.

That night Spareen selected from his mares the old, sickle-hocked one that was out of milk, for she was in heat. This mare he saddled and rode out into the steppe, far from the habitations of men into the Turk's territory. Finding a likely spot, he staked her out and instructed her to call to any nearby stallion.

The first to arrive was a coarse piebald which Spareen drove away. A few other scrubs came which Spareen also drove off, but finally Old Turk himself cantered in, his tail playing like a banner in the wind. The mare nickered seductively, and Old Turk came up and nosed her neck like a gentleman before mounting her from behind. When they had satisfied their desires, the Old Turk turned to go and put his foot right into the noose that Spareen had planted. He reared up and tried to fight the rope, but Spareen jumped up from his hiding place and got another rope around the Turk's rear legs. The great sovereign of the steppes stood helpless as a newborn foal while Spareen surveyed his prize.

Spareen was about to hobble the Turk and put a halter over that proud head, but found he just couldn't do it. It went against his Varkela way of thinking. Finally he untied the ropes and set the great stallion free.

"You must leave this part of the steppe," said Spareen. "For if you stay, Iskendar Khan will surely capture you, or put a bullet through your head trying. If you want to stay free, my advice to you is to leave this territory."

Old Turk snorted and shook out his magnificent mane. "If this is true, then I shall leave this place tonight, for to live is to run free."

◆ ◆ ◆

Spareen reported to the khan that his attempt had been unsuccessful. For the next few weeks he listened with guarded eyes to reports from Iskendar Khan's riders that the Turk was nowhere to be found.

When he confided in the golden-eyes mare, she broke her long silence to say, "You did rightly, Spareen."

"I'm glad you condescend to speak with me again," said Spareen. "I was getting lonely."

One night he was sitting outside his yurt, boiling up root of comfrey to make boneset tea, when Iskendar Khan's small, veiled wife came walking through the grass to find him.

"You must come," she said, "for my husband has not slept these last three nights on account of that horse, and I fear it is making him ill."

On hearing this, Spareen reached into his yurt and from his herbal preparations selected valerian root, skullcaps, hops, and chamomile. He carried these in his medicine bag as he followed Iskendar Khan's wife back to her husband's dwelling.

He found Iskendar Khan lying on a gold embroidered floor mat, his eyes bright with fever.

"I must find Old Turk," said the khan.

"But you must understand," said Spareen, "that a horse like that has a need to run free. I have spoken to him myself in the horse language, and I know it's true."

"But such a magnificent stud he would make," said the khan. "I must have him, and I will."

Spareen did not argue with the fire in Iskendar Khan's eye but busied himself making a sedative tea from boiled water. Within an hour the khan's eyelids drooped, and he fell into a deep slumber.

◆ ◆ ◆

It was a hungry summer for Spareen. Luckily for him, one of the Nogai tribe's sheep developed blackleg, and he found some employment that way, but as usual, they refused to take him on as their permanent leechman. Iskendar Khan got thinner and thinner is spite of an herbal carminative prepared by Spareen, and rich food prepared by the khan's wife.

One day Spareen heard a rumor that Old Turk had been spotted in the Caspian salt flats. That night when he returned from treating blackleg, he discovered that Iskendar's tent and all his rider' yurts had been removed. He knew what that meant.

In a week the khan returned with the Turk as his captive.

"As you can see, I took your advice, Spareen," said the khan. "I did not kill him, merely crippled him a little.'

Spareen examined Old Turk in his hastily thrown-up stall of mud and boards. The horse limped painfully on one leg.

"You will never run again," said Spareen. "Even if I were to set you free, you would not get far."

"If you set me free, I will run again, and I will show you how," said the proud old stallion.

Spareen suspected that he knew how. On an ink black night, dark as Spareen's hair, the leechman crept over to the horse pens of Iskendar Khan. It was no trick to witch the one guard on duty. Carefully, Spareen pried the boards out of the mud-and-wattle fence and led the Turk to freedom out on the steppe.

The Turk set off at a jerky trot—no more the free-swinging gait. Spareen followed at a distance on the golden-eyes mare. After a few days' journey they came to the salt flats and marshes of the Caspian. In the distance that deep green sea spanned the horizon. Old Turk followed a path that led up to a precipice overlooking the sea. Backing off, he lumbered into a canter, built up his speed, and leaped off the cliff. Spareen watched from below as the great horse galloped down a causeway of air to a watery death. Spareen sang the horse prayer over the waters, and the golden-eyes mare nickered a sad farewell. It was a long ride home.

A few nights later, as Spareen returned from a night's work, he saw a four-legged ghost dashing through the night over the silver bear-grass. At a whistle from Spareen the ghost horse slowed and came to touch noses with the golden-eyes mare, who flattened her ears and snapped, "I'm not in season, you young nape-nipper. Be gone!"

With a toss of silver mane, the young gray stallion

turned and galloped madly away until his hoof tattoo was lost in the sighing of the wind in the tall feather grass.

"Surely the son of his father," said Spareen, and his heart rejoiced that a scion of the old stock again ran free on the steppe.

"But what will you do about Varkura?" said the golden-eyes mare. "Although Iskendar Khan would have paid you well, I for one am glad you let Old Turk go."

"Varkura. . . ." mused Spareen smelling the scent of wild ginger in memory. "Never fear, I shall find a way."

"You will always say that, but so far you've been unsuccessful."

"Sometimes, Golden-eyes, I think you talk entirely too much," said Spareen.

# THE NEISSERIAN INVASION

THE INVADERS WERE susceptible to human diseases. Dr. Garth and I discovered this fact just twenty days after the invasion, when the first case of non-terrestrial gonorrhea came to our attention. Garth and I were in the Public Health Lab at the time, discussing the implications of the Serrabean takeover.

"Those bloody, blue devils will have us in serfdom, if things continue this way," says Dr. Garth, tugging at his stingy string of a mustache. He's referring to the subjugation of the U.S. Government to Serrabean control. The French had been the first to capitulate to the invader's demands, quickly followed by England, Russia, and the United Arab Republic.

"What choice do we have?" I pose a merely rhetorical question. The two attempts at resistance by the armed forces had been totally stopped by a telepathic control which the translators called "Non-Violent Mental Deprogramming."

"Apparently we will have to utilize non-violent means," muses Garth. "It's been done before successfully; remember Gandhi? And don't forget the civil disobedience to protest the Viet Nam war, back in the sixties." I think he might twist the wispy fringe right off his face.

"Who will start this hypothetical fifth column?" I wonder. "Not me. I'm not the heroic type. I'm just a humble public health officer."

At this point Lyla waves me over to the lab bench where she is working up cultures. Lyla's a sharp girl. I'm a little afraid of her in some ways. She has a way of looking at you that makes you feel sure she can see into that itching corner of your mind. That she knows with whom you copulate in dreams. Does she know how I long to fondle her chaste, gold maiden hair?

"It might interest a 'humble public health officer' to know that we have three new cases of resistant gonorrhea in this city," she says, dropping me at twenty paces with those deadly eyes. "While you two are solving the world's problems, life, love and lust go gaily onward."

I cross the room to where she sits flapping the lab slips at me.

"Here you are, Joe," she says, offering me three illegibly written lab reports.

"What does this mean?" I ask, pointing at what looks like 'Narwhll Threx' on one of the slips. "Your spelling must be getting worse."

"That's the patient's name," she replies, a bit defensively, I think.

"Oh, come off it, Lyla. Admit you goofed again."

"No, honestly. That's what Dr. Mailer wrote on the specimen. I copied it verbatim. Here, I'll show you." She digs into the pile of plastic cups by the stainless steel incinerator, sorts hopefully through the discards from yesterday, and comes up with one cupful of greenish gook. She triumphantly hands me the prize. "Narwhll Threx."

"Terrific!" I spout. "I get to interview the Yugoslavian ambassador."

"My God, Joe!" exclaims Dr. Garth. "It's a Serrabean name. That patient is an alien." He's getting that intensely thoughtful look in his methylene blue eyes. I recognize that beatific stare. It means another research project: twenty more embarrassing questions for me to put to those unhappy souls before we inoculate their clappy bottoms with Ultracillin."

Lyla sighs. She knows that stare means twenty more agar plates for her to inoculate and read each day.

◆ ◆ ◆

Neisseria gonorrhea, a most insidious little microbe, is identified clinically by its characteristic moist gray colonies on chocolate agar. It stubbornly refuses to grow at temperatures above or below 35 degrees Centigrade, approximately normal body heat. A finicky organism, it requires 5 percent $CO_2$ on primary isolation. It cannot live outside the body for more than four hours, and only invades the mucous membranes, which precludes one's getting it from toilet seats.

◆ ◆ ◆

I climb out of the sky-cycle and meander slowly through the bazaar of New Ankara. The high rise slum reaches nearly half a mile overhead in serpentine towers of arabesque symmetry. Blue kites fly above the onion dome mosque. Turkish immigrants have taken over what used to be Harlem. (The anatolian plateau is now a wasted tract of radioactive debris.)

I fumble through my notebook and find the address. An elevator door sucks open to take me in. On the 53rd floor, I find number 890: Oya Solent, 29, Ethnologist.

The door opens and a pleasant-looking woman with dark Turkoman eyes and hair listens to my spiel with quiet horror.

"It's my duty to inform you. . . .

"Positive culture . . . Neisseria gonorrhea. . . .

"Must receive injections of Ultracillin within three days. . . .

"Must attend prophylaxis classes or suffer status demotion."

◆ ◆ ◆

The classes have improved things a lot. And with the threat of status demotion, we get fewer than ten percent repeat offenders.

"Names of all sexual contact within the last two months. . . ."

I'm used to it, the long pause. . . . The abashed silence as the mind trips back over the last sixty days' peccadillos.

◆ ◆ ◆

"None," she states with cryptic assurance.

My left eyebrow creeps upward skeptically.

"It's true," she hurries on. "My husband and I have been separated for three months and there's been no one else."

"It's important to name your contacts," I remonstrate, "to prevent spread of a harmful disease, and if you refuse," I deliver the kicker, "it is automatic status demotion."

"But I'm telling the truth," she insists. The dark eyes plead.

I ask one of Dr. Garth's new questions. "Any alien contacts?"

Puzzled frown.

"Not in that way, but I'm on the Serrabean Project through Attaturk College. The aliens can get it?"

"Apparently. What sort of contact do you have with them? Any use of the same eating utensils?" I ask.

"No. What about toilet seats? We use the same facilities."

I am disappointed at this tired old cliché. I mark her down for demotion and terminate the interview.

◆ ◆ ◆

In the moist, dark places of the body, concealed in folds of skin and mucous membrane, here the Neisserians invade. On the gram stain of pus or other body fluids, one sees innocent looking pairs of pink, coffee bean shaped cocco-bacilli. These fill the polymorphonuclear cells until they burst into raspberry-like globules.

◆ ◆ ◆

I skycycle across town to Attaturk College for the next case on my itinerary.

Case two. Dr. Mobius Mular, 48, anthropologist.

He is not particularly happy to invite me into his study. On the dark, mahogany walls hang large hookah pipes, complete with rubber tubing and glass, water-filled chambers through which smoke bubbles. I wonder if he is addicted to nicotine. Some of these Anth-Soc types have funny archaic practices.

Dr. Mular is divorced and claims to have had no sexual contacts within the last six months. I can't believe it! Two in one day. Do I get more than my share of liars, or have puritan sentiments made a comeback?

◆ ◆ ◆

Case three. Narwhll Threx, Serrabean, age unknown, sex: presumptive male.

I have been putting this off until last, I realize, partly

because I have enough hangups about asking humans about their intimate lives. With an alien, how does one begin? Especially if the alien is an overlord usurper on one's native planet.

At my knock the door slides open and a large blue being peers out at me from two little eyes at the end of a trunk-like proboscis.

I suppress a momentary shudder at the expanse of viscous surface and wonder how any human could desire closeness with a Serrabean. This response is short-lived, and I am overwhelmed with a wave of such unconditional love as must accompany religious experiences. The moistness is no longer repugnant, but altogether charming. So this is "Non-Violent Mental Deprogramming."

"It is my duty to inform you that a positive culture for Neisseria gonorrhea has grown out of your specimen taken the third of this month."

The trunk waves slowly and perhaps a little sadly from side to side.

"Then I have the Human disease?" says a voice which echos like a taped recording through a hollow pipe.

◆ ◆ ◆

Gonorrhea, when first reported in Europe in the 1500s, was called "the French disease" by the English. The French obligingly passed the blame on to the Spanish, who named it "the Italian disease." Now the Serrabeans will call it "the Human disease."

◆ ◆ ◆

Narwhll denies any sexual contact with humans and rather abruptly dismisses me. The door slides closed with a *shoosh*. I wonder if I have offended him. Perhaps they have taboos against miscegenation. The mental fix wears off and I make my exit wondering how any human could possibly get laid with one of these slimy humanoid slugs. I would rather fornicate with an octopus.

Dr. Garth reads my report with interest. "So no one will 'fess up' to sexual contact with an alien. And two of our clients are associated with the University project on Serrabean language and culture. Perhaps we should check out the project and see what goes on there. Take cultures on everything. Say it's for a special study, and in your discreet way try to find the sexual contact. She's very important."

"How do you know it's a she?" I ask. "After all, they *are* bisexual hermaphrodites, aren't they? Why couldn't it just as well be a male contact?"

"Because the invaders are all going through their male phase, if I'm not mistaken. Their sex changes during the course of their lifetime; the younger phase being male, the adult, female."

"You mean we've been invaded by a bunch of adolescent boys?"

"Essentially," says Dr. Garth. "If they have the usual sexual curiosity of adolescent males, it's not unlikely that one of them may have experimented with a human female."

"Tremendous! If we find her and encourage her, maybe we can start an epidemic and wipe out these Serrabeans." I'm just being sarcastic, but Dr. Garth gets that funny, distant look in his eye.

"That *would* be one form of non-violent intervention," he says, absently tugging at his mustache.

◆ ◆ ◆

Neisseria gonorrhea, on incubation, in vitro, grows slowly at best and may take as long as three days to produce a sprinkling of small, mucoid, gray dots against the brown agar background. In vivo it may produce symptoms in a few days, lie dormant for a month, or may produce no symptoms at all as it does irreparable damage.

◆ ◆ ◆

The next day I go to Attaturk College and take cultures. I culture eating utensils, cups, food and, yes, even toilet seats. The Serrabeans have their own bathroom facilities and it is there that I first see non-terran pornographic art. The subject, a male, portrayed in indelible blue ink on the stall door, waving its multiple phalli in the air, looks for all the world like a walrus head with a mouth full of eels. On the adjacent wall I see what I suppose to be a female of the species straddling another walrus. "Well, there's no accounting for taste," I mutter and set about probing the intimate surfaces of the toilet seat with cotton swabs dipped in nutrient gel agar. By the time I'm finished I've worked up a sweat. The interior of this Serrabean toilet is as hot and humid as a Turkish bath. They must have some phobia about sitting on a cold potty. All the windows are fogged with moisture.

◆ ◆ ◆

Back at the lab Dr. Garth has news for me.

"There are six new alien cultures," he says, handing me the slips. There are also two new human cultures—positives—both from the College. Upon following up these cultures, I find that all the aliens and one of the human contacts deny any sexual activity whatsoever.

The next day I talk with Garth again about this peculiar turn of events.

"Perhaps we had better revise our hypothesis. Maybe the contact is non-venereal in origin," he says.

"But you know that's highly unlikely," I say.

"But the possibility exists."

"All the cases I've ever run into, the patient eventually admitted to some form of sexual contact," I answer.

Lyla stops me in the hall.

"You don't buy Dr. Garth's theory," she says, reading my face.

"Not when he goes off on this non-venereal kick. The day I see a non-venereal case of gonorrhea, I'll eat my jock strap."

"What about an infant born to an infected mother?"

She *is* right. Babies used to contract the disease, usually in the eyes, while passing through the infected birth canal. The eyes would cloud up for a few days and then the buggies would migrate elsewhere leaving blindness in their wake. I've never seen a case. Nowadays all doctors treat newborns' eyes with drops of silver nitrate solution to prevent this tragedy.

◆ ◆ ◆

That afternoon I finally find our girl, a coed from Attaturk College.

She comes to the door in a dressing gown, a sandy blond with fat cheeks. She looks like a chipmunk when she smiles. She stands there with a bag of peanuts in hand and continues to munch all through the interview.

"Yeah, I fucked one of those blue bastards; what of it?" She shells a few more peanuts and stuffed them into her cheek pouches.

"And when did this occur?"

"About two weeks ago."

I check my memory. That would be about right.

"It's not illegal is it?" she asks.

"Only if you don't name your contacts," I say.

"I wish these Serrabean would go home."

"So do I, but there's not much we can do about it."

"The trouble with these aliens," she says, "is that even

though I hate them, when they're around I love them. I can't help myself."

"That's the NVDP," I say.

"What?"

"Non-Violent Mental Deprogramming. It makes it impossible to will them harm. If only there were some means of resistance. . . ." Then I remember Dr. Garth's non-violent method.

"Make love, not war," I say.

"What do you mean?" she asks.

"Just this. Your infection doesn't need to be treated immediately. If you could get laid with more Serrabeans before we treat you, it would be a service to Humankind."

◆ ◆ ◆

That next week the Serrabean gonorrhea epidemic increases. Their scientists have no knowledge of how to treat the disease, and many come to the clinic for Ultracillin injections. As fast as we can treat them, they keep coming in, lines of blue Serrabeans dressed down to those little tunics they wear in lieu of BVDs. Infection of a Serrabean is painful to behold. The milky streaming discharge. The roseate fuschia buboes that swarm over loins and thighs. The phalli dwindling to earthworm proportions. Serrabean are vulnerable over their whole body surface, it being a modified mucous membrane.

◆ ◆ ◆

I tell Dr. Garth about my talk with the girl with alien contact. "Apparently my pep talk with her had quite an effect."

"I wouldn't be so quick to claim the glory, Joe," says Garth. "Most of them insist they had no human contact and we are still getting human patients from Attaturk College who claim no sexual contacts."

◆ ◆ ◆

A mystery, but I'm still convinced that sexual contact is the culprit, and increase my pressure in questioning the people I'm sent out to interview.

The next day when I'm out at Attaturk College, following up more cases, human and Serrabean, Dr. Garth telephones and has me paged.

"Have you heard the news?" he asks. "The Serrabean leader issued a statement today. Apparently they are disgusted with our venereal disease-ridden planet. They are evacuating and declaring it off limits."

I agree to meet him for a drink later to celebrate. I still have cases to interview and I go back to work with a vengeance.

"Sexual contact within the last two months."

"None." Dark Turkoman eyes regard me hostily. Oya Solent again. She had been treated, released and gotten reinfected and she still expects me to believe she's as pure as the Virgin Mary. I mark her down for another demotion.

Before going back to the lab, I make a pit stop in the bathroom. I have to use the Serrabean facilities because of some problem with the college plumbing. Serrabean toilets are shaped wrong and give the human butt a rather awkward ride.

◆ ◆ ◆

Later that day, Dr. Garth reads my reports and smiles over my observations about the truthfulness of my clients.

"So you still think Mrs. Solent is lying about her contacts," he says. "Well, I have some evidence which leads me to believe that you owe that lady an apology. You see, we finally grew out some positive cultures from those Serrabean toilets. It seems their bathrooms are heated at

37 degrees Centigrade and the moisture and $CO_2$ concentration are just right to harbor N. Gonorrhea. Though that girl may have started it, this is one case where the infection did get spread by toilet seats.

◆ ◆ ◆

As I listen to this discourse, I'm plagued with an itching sensation in my crotch which I barely restrain myself from scratching. How the mighty are fallen!

The symptoms appear three days later. I'm pissing pink crud and it hurts like hell. Down at the lab Dr. Garth checks me over and I find myself wishing that you could still go to private doctors to be treated for VD. I'm horribly chagrined to have Garth dabbing at my weeping genitals with a cotton swab. The gram stain is positive and I nearly pass out when I see them coming at me with a needle large enough to house a small drill bit.

"I do believe the Neisserians have invaded," chuckles Dr. Garth as I struggle back into my pants.

◆ ◆ ◆

But the worst part is I will never have the courage to ask Lyla for a date after she reads my positive culture.

# SPIDERSONG

Brenneker, the lyre spider, lived inside a lute, a medieval instrument resembling a pear-shaped guitar. The lute was an inexpensive copy of one made by an old master and had rosewood walls and a spruce sounding board. Her home was sparsely furnished, a vast expanse of unfinished wood, a few sound pegs reaching from floor to ceiling like Greek columns, and in one corner, near the small F-shape sound holes, the fantasy of iron-silk thread that was Brenneker's web. Brenneker's home was an unusual one for a lyre spider. Most of them spin their webs in hollow tawba stalks, which echo the music of these tiny fairy harps seldom heard by ears of men. Lyre spiders play duets with each other, sometimes harmonizing, sometimes bouncing counterpoint melodies back and forth across the glades between the tall bamboo-like tawba. They play their webs to attract prey, to win a mate, or for the sheer joy of music. They live alone except for the few weeks in mother's silken egg case and one day of spiderlings climbing up the tawba to cast their threads into the wind and fly away. When they mate, the enbrace lasts but a few moments. Then the female eats the male, who gives himself gladly to this deepest union of two souls.

Originally, Brenneker had lived in the forest, surrounded by music of her own kind. Although she lived alone, she was never lonely, for she could always hear the mandolin-like plucking of Twinklebright, her nearest neighbor, the deep, droning chords of old Birdslayer, and occasionally the harpsichord tones of Klavier, carried on the breeze.

One hot afternoon as Brenneker experimented with augmented fifths, she noticed that some of her neighbors had stopped midsong. She suddenly realized she was the only one still playing and she stopped abruptly, leaving a leading tone hanging on the air like an unfinished sentence.

"These ones should do," she heard a man's voice say. An angry blow struck the base of her tawba stalk. She felt herself falling as the tawba that was her home broke at the base, tumbling her to the floor of the glade below. Bruised and frightened, she scampered quickly back inside her home and clung to her silent, broken web. She felt herself lifted up and then dropped with a jar as her tawba was tossed into a wagon.

Over many hours of jolting and rattling, she fell asleep, and when she awoke, all was quiet and dark. She climbed out of her stalk and began to explore her new surroundings, a workbench with many hollow wooden objects lying about. Although she had never seen a musical instrument such as men make, she recognized with the eye of a musician that their shape was intended to give sound. She chose a lute and squeezed her plump body through one of the soundholes, saying, "Certainly this will give greater tone than my old home." She began to string her web.

At night there was no music in the instrument maker's shop, and she was lonely without the songs of her friends to cheer her. Since she was also hungry, she played her hunger song, and a fat, stupid moth came, aching to be devoured. When she'd finished with him, she tossed his powdery wings out the sound hole.

In the morning, the old instrument maker, Sanger, came to open up his shop. He paused in the shop doorway rattling his keys and then turned on the overhead light. Brenneker watched him from the sound holes of her new home as he ran a wrinkled hand through his sparse, gray hair, stuffed his keys back into a deep pocket, and picked a viola from the wall. Carefully, he adjusted the tuning of the strings, and then, picking up the bow, he played a short, lilting tune and then replaced the instrument on its peg on the wall. He made his way along the wall, pausing at each instrument to check the tuning. When he came to Brenneker's lute, he did the same, tightening the strings briefly and then playing a few bars of melody. Brenneker felt her whole surroundings vibrate with the tone and her web pulsed in sympathetic vibration. Timidly, she picked out a few notes of the song.

"Odd," said Mr. Sanger. "I'd never noticed that it had such lovely overtones. Too bad I had to use such cheap materials in its construction." He placed the lute back on the wall and was about to pick up a zither, when the shop bell rang to announce that someone had come in from the street.

A young girl and her father came through the door and paused to look at the violins.

"But I don't want to play violin," said the girl, who was about ten years old. "Everyone plays violin. I want something different."

"Well, what about a guitar?" said her father. "Your friend Marabeth plays one quite well. It seems like a proper instrument for a young lady."

"But that's just it," said the girl, whose name Brenneker later found out was Laurel. "I don't want to copycat someone else. I want an instrument that isn't played by just anyone. I want something special."

Sanger interrupted this conversation to say, "Have you considered the lute?" He removed Brenneker's home from the wall and strummed a chord. The vibration in the web tickled Brenneker's feet as she strummed the same chord an octave higher.

"What a lovely tone it has!" said Laurel, touching the strings and plucking them one by one.

"Be careful," said her father. "That's an antique."

"Not so," said Sanger. "It's a copy. Made it myself. And I intended it to be played, not just looked at like a dusty old museum piece."

"May I try?" asked the girl. Sanger gave the instrument to her and she sat down on a stool, placing the lute across her lap. She strummed a discord which caused Brenneker to flinch and grip her strings tightly so they wouldn't sound.

"Let me show you how," said the instrument maker. "Put your first finger in that fret and your middle finger there, like so." He indicated where the fingers should fret the strings to make a chord. Laurel plucked the strings one by one. The tone was tinny but true. The second time she plucked, Brenneker plucked inside, on her own instrument. Rich, golden tones emanated from the lute.

"Oh, Father, this is the instrument for me," said Laurel.

"But who will teach you to play such an antiquated instrument?

"I would be glad to," said Sanger. "I have studied medieval and Renaissance music and I would like to share it with an interested pupil."

"Please, Father?"

"Well, perhaps . . . there is the question of cost. I can't afford a very expensive instrument," said her father.

"This lute, although made with loving care and much skill," said Sanger, "is unfortunately made of inexpensive wood, and for that reason it is very reasonably priced."

Mr. Sanger and Laurel's father were able to make agreeable terms for the lute and the cost of lessons. That morning Laurel took the lute, Brenneker and all, home with her.

The first few weeks of lessons were torture for Brenneker, who sat huddled, clenching her strings to her body to damp them. But as Laurel improved, Brenneker rewarded her by playing in unison. This was great incentive to Laurel, who did not realize that she was only partial author of the lovely music. Mr. Sanger was himself at a loss to explain how such beautiful tones came from such a cheaply built instrument. He did not credit his workmanship, although this was in some measure responsible, but told Laurel that the lute was haunted by a fairy harpist, and he advised her to leave a window open at night and put out a bowl of milk and honey before she went to bed. Perhaps he had been the beneficiary of such a fairy in the past, for Brenneker found that the milk and the open window provided her with a bountiful supply of flies and insects, which she tempted by song through the sound holes of the lute to make her supper.

Sanger valued highly the virtue of two playing in harmony. "For the ability to blend with another in duet is the mark of maturity in a true musician," he would say. "Harmony between two players recaptures for us briefly that time when the universe was young, untainted by evil, and the morning stars sang together."

Brenneker never played by herself unless she was sure that she was alone. She played when Laurel played or at night when everyone was sleeping. When spring came that year, she played the mating song and waited, but no lover came. The next night she tried again, this time varying the song by adding trills, but still no one came. Brenneker tried for several nights before she finally admitted to herself that there was no fault in her song, but that none of her folk dwelt in this faraway land and so there was no one to answer. But this reasoning made her feel unhappy, and she preferred to think that it might be some imperfections in her song, which could be righted by practice.

As Laurel grew older, Brenneker noticed that the quality of their music changed. Whereas she had formerly been a lover of sprightly dance tunes, Laurel became more interested in old ballads and would sing as she accompanied herself on the lute. One of her favorites was "Barbara Allen," another, "The Wife of Ushers Well."

She was often asked to perform at weddings and parties. She met other lovers of medieval music and even other lute players. Laurel would sometimes allow others to play her instrument, which drew a mixed response. If Brenneker knew the tune of the strange artist, she would pick along. If not, she held her strings silent, leaving the others to wonder how Laurel got such rounded tones while they only strummed dull, tinny notes.

One summer evening Laurel took a blanket, the lute and Brenneker to a woodsy place and sat down alone to play. She sang many of the old ballads and then she would stop for a while and listen. Then she would play another song. Brenneker wondered at this until she heard answering notes from a recorder in a grove nearby. The two instruments played a duet, with occasional counterpoint melody, and then the recorder player drew near, and Brenneker saw that it was a young man.

"Aha," she thought, "Laurel plays to attract a mate."

The young man sat down beside Laurel on the grass.

"I knew you'd come," he said to her.

She moved over toward him and he put an arm around her waist and kissed her.

This went on for quite some time. After a while the two said good-bye, and Laurel picked up her blanket and trudged homeward, while her love went in the other direction.

◆ ◆ ◆

"Strange," thought Brenneker. "She did not eat him." This bothered the lyre spider until she stopped to reflect; "Birds do not eat their mates. Perhaps the humans are like birds, but I had always thought them more intelligent than that."

A few nights later, Laurel took her blanket and went to the grove again. The young man, whose name was Thomas, was there waiting for her. They played a few songs and then they made love. As she walked home, Laurel sang "Barbara Allen."

"And still she does not eat him," thought Brenneker. "Their way of being together is different from ours. Yet I'm sure it must mean as much to them as ours does to us. Yet it seems so incomplete. Impermanent."

The presence of the human lovers made Brenneker more aware of her own loneliness. "If I could mate," she thought, "I would make the most beautiful egg-sack all of silk, and my eggs would sway to the music of the lute until they hatched. Then they would fly to neighboring trees and build their own lyres and play to me and I wouldn't be alone anymore." But when she played her love songs, softly on the night air, no lover came. She was used to it by now, but she never gave up hope.

One evening the two lovers had a quarrel.

"You must marry me this fall," Thomas insisted.

"But we have no money," Laurel objected. "You are only an apprentice of your trade, and it will be a long time before you bring home a journeyman's wage. I would not be able to go to the university to study music."

"We would get by somehow," said Thomas. "You could take in music students and teach the lute. We could pick up a little extra money playing for gatherings."

"But I do so much want to go to the university," said Laurel. "We could go to the city and both take jobs. That way we could be together and I could study for my degree."

"I can't get as good a job in the city as here," said Thomas, "and besides, you could not earn enough to support yourself and pay tuition. So you might as well settle here with me."

"There has to be a way for me to continue my study of music," said Laurel, "and I intend to find it."

When Thomas left, he did not kiss Laurel goodbye.

Laurel, thoughtful and concerned, put her lute aside and went to bed early. She did not forget to leave a window open, however, or set out milk to feed the fairy. Brenneker pondered their dilemma and could see no solution. While she was brooding over this, she heard the unmistakable sound of a lyre spider tuning up its instrument, and this caused her to listen intently. It was a curious song, having a haunting quality, a shadowing of minor key but not quite. This was no spider song, Brenneker was sure, but it was definitely played by one of her own kind. She strummed an answering chord and the other player stopped in midphrase as if startled. Brenneker played part of an old song she'd played many times at home. The other answered her with the refrain of the song, and so they played back and forth for a while until the other stopped. Brenneker was somewhat disappointed that the song had ended, but a few moments later she discovered why. A gentle tapping on the sounding board roused her attention and she went to the F holes to peer out. The other spider, a male, had followed her music and had come to investigate. He clambered up the side of the instrument to her vantage point.

"How lovely," he said, "to hear the songs of home in a strange land. Tell me, Lady, how did you come here?"

"By accident," said Brenneker. "The humans picked my tawba stalk for a flute and brought me here. But I have never seen another of our kind here until now."

"I came in similar fashion," said the male. "My name is Wisterness, and, until now, I had thought I was the only one of our kind that had ranged so widely."

"What was that strange tune you played? Is it in a minor key? I have heard none like it before," said Brenneker.

"It's neither major or minor," said Wisterness. "It is based on a modal scale like some of the Renaissance music I've heard you play. I've noticed that you sometimes play in the Dorian mode, which is somewhat similar. Actually, I was playing a southern mountain tune called 'June Apple.' The tuning is called 'mountain minor,' or 'A to G' tuning among them, but it is actually the older double-tonic scale, based on the highland bagpipe tuning, or, according to some sources, the Irish Harp."

"My goodness," said Brenneker, "you certainly know a lot about music. I haven't heard half of those words. I do remember playing 'Scarborough Fair' in the Dorian mode, but that's about the extent of my music theory."

"I may know more theory, but you are the better musician, Lady. I am always barely learning one tune and then going on to something new. Consequently my playing lacks polish. I have listened to your songs for several nights before summoning the courage to answer."

"I certainly have no complaint against your playing," said Brenneker. "I thought it was quite beautiful. I am curious about one thing, though, and that is your age. I never knew male spiders lived much more than a few years, yet you seem quite mature and well-read. Have you never mated?"

Wisterness shuffled his pedipalps and appeared slightly embarrassed.

"No, I never have," he said. "There was one once in my youth that I cared for, but she chose to devour another. Then one day I followed a woodsman to listen to his song, and I was carried off in a load of wood and eventually came to this place. Since then I have devoted myself to the study of humans and their music, but it has been lonely at times."

Since it was not the mating time, Wisterness left after awhile and went back to his lyre, which was strung in a hollow tree not far from the window, and he and Brenneker played duets most of the night. But sometimes she paused to listen to the piercing modal sweetness of Wisterness, as he experimented with different tunings from the lonely southern mountains.

◆ ◆ ◆

The next morning, Laurel did not sit down to her music at the usual time, but instead put on her coat and went out with a purposeful look in her eyes. The next day, at the practice hour, a younger girl came to Laurel's door carrying a lute under her arm, and Laurel taught her a lesson. It was "Greensleeves," a favorite of Brenneker's, and she played along at first, but the student had troubles, and they kept stopping mid-verse and starting over until Brenneker decided it was more pain than pleasure and gave it up. Before the student left, she counted out a small sum of money which Laurel put in a large jar on her dresser. This money, Brenneker learned, was to go toward Laurel's university tuition.

As the weeks passed, more students came, until Laurel had five beginners to teach. One student came twice a week from a distant township. Sanger, the old instrument maker, still came by once in a while to teach Laurel a song, but she had long ago surpassed him in musical skill, and he never charged for his "lessons" anymore.

His fingers had grown arthritic and he could not play as well as he had in the past. He no longer took students, which made Laurel one of the few teachers of the lute in her part of the country. The money piled up slowly in the jar, but it was nowhere near enough, and sometimes Brenneker would overhear Laurel arguing with her father at night about her plans to go to the university.

"Even if you could get a degree in music," he would say, "that doesn't guarantee that you'll be able to support yourself. Why not study something practical that you can find a good job in?"

Laurel agreed to take courses in handicrafts and midwifery to pacify her father, whom she still depended upon for support, but her heart belonged to music, and she refused to give up her plans for further study.

When she saw Thomas now, they both avoided talking about future plans, as this always provoked a fight, and he did not come to see her as often. Brenneker fretted about this, as she saw Laurel suffering in silence. When Laurel played, Brenneker sometimes wove her mating song into the web of sound hoping that Thomas would hear and return to renew his love. But he did not hear, or if he did, he didn't come.

One warm spring night, Brenneker alone played her mating song hopefully to the open window, and after a short time Wisterness came, tapping shyly on her sound box to announce his presence.

"You must come out," he said, "for the sound holes are too small for me to get in."

Brenneker had failed to recognize her predicament. As a young spider, she had entered through the holes with ease, but now she was bigger, and therefore trapped within the lute. She forced her legs out the F holes, and she could feel the tantalizing closeness of his belly fur, but try as they might, they could not negotiate across the wooden barrier.

Finally he said, "Brenneker, I fear our love must go unconsummated, for you can't get out and I can't get in. But then perhaps it's better that way, for even if we could somehow manage to mate, we could not partake of the deeper sharing, with you in there and me out here."

And so he left sadly. She did not hear his song for several days, and then one day the wind carried the distant strains of "Billy in the Lowground" to her window. The sad Irish mode echoing in the lonely Appalachian melody, told her that he had moved his harp farther away to avoid the pain of their unsatisfied need. He was too far to answer any of her musical questions or play the counterpoint games.

One day Laurel invited Thomas over to her home. She was very anxious to share a piece of news with him.

"The university is offering a music scholarship," she said. "There will be a contest and I intend to participate. If I win, my tuition would be paid, and if we both found jobs, we could be together while I go to school in the city."

Thomas thought about this before answering and then said, "It's not the money that really bothers me, it's your attitude. I get the feeling that I am not as important to you as your music. I want you to be happy, but I don't wish to play second fiddle to a lute."

"But my work is as important to me as yours is to

you," said Laurel. "The truth is that neither of us wish to make the sacrifice of our career goals to be with the other."

"I had hoped our love meant more to you than your music," said Thomas, "but I see I was wrong."

"It means equally as much to me," said Laurel. "I just don't think I should be the one to have to make the sacrifice of my career. There is no reason you couldn't get a job in the city. It would not be forever, only a few years. Then we could come back here and you could take up where you left off."

"I don't see it that way," he said. "In a few years I would be behind everyone in my training and I'd be competing with younger men whom they don't have to pay as much. If I stay, I have opportunity for advancement in a few years."

"Well, I suppose we will part then, when the summer's over," said Laurel. "I shall miss you terribly, but that's the way things work out sometimes. There is one last request I want to make of you, and that is, will you accompany my playing when I go to the contest?"

"I'm afraid I can't do that," said Thomas. "It would be adding insult to injury if I participated in the very thing that takes you away from me."

After Thomas left, Laurel cried. She went to bed early and even forgot about the milk for the fairy. This did not disturb Brenneker very much, for she had lost her appetite listening to their argument. She was pondering Laurel's problem in her mind (it seemed strange that humans could have barriers to love more complex than her wooden cage) when she heard a strange grinding noise as of a small drill emanating from one corner of the lute. She scampered to the source of the sound and stood watching the smooth surface of the unfinished wood as the sound came nearer. Suddenly a little bump appeared in the surface, and then the bump dissolved in a small pile of sawdust, and an ugly bulbish head poked out of the newly formed hole. Brenneker pounced at the woodworm but missed as it pulled back into its tunnel. Frustrated, she stood tapping at the hole with her forelegs, as the worm withdrew and burrowed in a different direction.

"You must leave," said Brenneker to the worm. "You are destroying my home and Laurel's lute."

"There is plenty of wood here for both of us," came the muffled reply of the woodworm. "You may have the rosewood, and I'll eat only the spruce."

"But I don't eat wood," said Brenneker, "and you shouldn't eat this lute. There is plenty of other wood that you can eat. Leave my home alone. You are destroying a musical instrument. Have you no appreciation for music?"

"Hmm, yes, music," said the worm, whose name was Turkawee. "I've never cared for that funny-sounding stuff. Leave it to the birds, I always say."

"You ignorant barbarian!" exclaimed Brenneker.

"I think spiders are more barbaric than our kind," said Turkawee, "for spiders eat their cousins the insects, and even their own mates. You should take care whom you go calling a barbarian."

"Philistine, then!" snorted Brenneker. "You obviously have no concept of a higher culture than your own."

"Culture, you say?" said Turkawee. "That's a term my snooty Aunt Beetle used to use. She was always admiring the wings of butterflies. She knew an artist who made pictures of the wings. She ended up stuck with a pin to a cork board because all her interest in culture led her to follow a butterfly too closely into a collector's net. Culture is also for the birds, I say."

Brenneker, having no answer for this, retreated to her web and played the angriest song she could think of, which was a military march. The worm ignored her and continued gnawing at the wood of the lute.

Two days later, Brenneker was surveying the damage done by Turkawee. She was dismayed to find one part of the sounding board completely riddled with holes. She set about to mend it, binding the remaining wood with the steely white thread that she extruded from her spinnerets. The patch was actually quite strong, perhaps more so than the surrounding wood, but the discrepancy in the surface weakened the instrument structurally. The tension of the lute strings could cause the instrument to break, if the patch didn't hold.

Brenneker returned to her web by the sound posts and fell asleep. She wasn't used to making so much new thread, and the effort had drained her strength. In the night when she awoke, she called many insects to her supper with song, for she was ravenously hungry due to her exertion. The next day when Laurel tuned up the lute to play for a wedding, Brenneker noted with satisfaction that the patch held. But the ravages of the woodworm continued.

Old Sanger, the instrument maker, when he heard that Laurel intended to enter the scholarship contest, came by the house to offer his advice. He had played in competition in the past, and he knew what sort of artistry was apt to attract the notice of the judges and what displays of skill might sway their opinion.

"It is always a good idea to include in your repertoire a few songs that are not well known and played by everyone. And in the songs that are better known, try to display some different interpretation or more rare harmony. A few classical pieces in your presentation are in order, and playing a duet, or having someone accompany you is essential; so be sure to play your arrangement of 'The Ash Grove' with that young-man friend of yours. Your counterpoint harmony mixes very well with his recorder, and such a presentation will be sure to impress the judges. They will be looking for that particular blending of tones that displays your sense of harmony not only with your partner but with yourself and the universe."

"Poor Laurel," thought Brenneker. "What will she do without Thomas' accompaniment?"

Laurel said nothing to Sanger about her falling out with Thomas, and after he left she practiced "The Ash Grove" unaccompanied and tried to develop some new variations on the old theme. Brenneker was tempted to play the recorder part, but since to do so would reveal her presence, she contented herself with her usual practice of playing in unison or one octave higher than the melody.

That night Brenneker made a tour of the inside of her home and found that the woodworm had damaged the bond where the neck of the lute joins the body. She set about to repair the damage as best she could, plugging the holes with spidersilk and binding the weakened seam with long, tough strands. It was hard work and took much of her strength. She could barely stay awake long enough to eat the cricket that came chirping to hear her music.

Finally the greatly anticipated day came and Laurel took the coach to the big city where the contest was to be held. She refused to surrender her lute to the baggage rack and carried it in her lap, where it provoked much comment among the other passengers.

"What is that strange instrument?" they would ask. Or, "Please play us a tune."

Laurel consented and filled the coach with dulcet tones as her clear voice transported all the listeners to "Scarborough Fair."

When they arrived in the city, Laurel spent some of her hard-earned lesson money on a room at the inn. That night when Laurel was asleep, Brenneker found more holes to fill. Turkawee had almost destroyed one of the interior braces of the frame. And not only that, but also he had eaten away most of the surface below the bridge. If this were to give way, the strings would go slack and the instrument would be unplayable. Brenneker worked far into the night, binding the lute with her webbing. So far her spider silk, being stronger in tensile strength than steel wire of its same proportions, had held the lute together. But Brenneker was worried that the damage was too extensive. The inside of the lute was completely webbed and re-webbed in silk and she knew it would not hold forever. She ate sparsely that night of the few insects that inhabit an inn and then forced her body to make more thread to continue the repairs. By daybreak she was nearly exhausted. She tried to get some sleep but Laurel woke early, concerned about the contest, and practiced her pieces, causing Brenneker to get no sleep at all.

Brenneker dozed on the carriage trip across town to the university but awoke in time to restring and tune her musical web before the contest began.

Both Brenneker and Laurel fidgeted nervously as they awaited their turn to play. There were many contestants, including a few lutists. One young man held the very antique instrument of which Laurel's was a copy. He allowed Laurel to stroke the strings once to demonstrate the superiority of its sound. But he was quite impressed when Laurel strummed a few bars on her own instrument with Brenneker's lyre in tandem. "I don't understand it," he said. "Your cheaply made modern instrument sounds almost as good as mine."

"Better," thought Brenneker, smugly, but then she remembered the damaged bridge and hoped it would stand the strain. She roused herself wearily and went to find a few more holes which she hastily filled with silk.

When Laurel's time came to play, she mounted a stool on the edge of the stage. Brenneker peered out through the sound holes and saw a sea of faces watching. As Laurel tuned up, Brenneker heard an unnerving creak as the wood near the bridge shifted slightly. To her horror she saw daylight between the bridge and the body of the lute. She jumped to the ceiling of her home, bound the gap quickly, and prayed that the mend would hold. Her spinnerets ached with the strain of making so much silk, and she was very tired, but forced herself to pick the strings nimbly as Laurel began with a lively dance tune. Apparently the lovely tone impressed the judges, for Laurel was selected from a large field of competition to enter the finals.

The young man with the antique instrument was also one of the finalists, and he stopped to wish Laurel good luck. Laurel asked him if he would accompany her on "The Ash Grove," but he excused himself, saying that time would be too short for him to learn the intricate counterpart melody. He also assured her that without a duet piece, she didn't have a chance in the competition.

This point was emphasized by the lovely duet played by the young man and a woman who accompanied him on the psaltry. They received a standing ovation from the audience and high marks from the judges.

"Mercy," thought Brenneker. "Now Laurel won't be able to win the scholarship," and spider tears dampened the silk of her web.

"Hey! It's raining on my picnic," said a small voice near her.

She looked over and saw Turkawee calmly munching on a piece of spruce.

Without thinking, Brenneker pounced and bit with just enough venom to cause the woodworm to fall into a swoon.

"That should keep you from doing more damage!" she snapped. But the damage had already been done. One of the sounding pegs looked as if it were ready to crumble into dust. Brenneker could feel, through her feet, the ominous vibrations as the tension of the strings pulled against the ravaged wood.

Finally Laurel's turn came again. She played a few classical pieces, a rondo, and sang "The Wife of Ushers Well," accompanying herself beautifully with an intricate rhythm she had worked out. For her last song, she began "The Ash Grove." Her first variation was neatly composed, but Brenneker thought it lacked the clever harmony of the previous duet. The second variation sounded very lonely without accompaniment, and this provoked Brenneker to try something she'd never done before. On the third verse she began to play her web in the counterpoint harmony as she had heard Thomas play so many times on the recorder. Laurel paused abruptly, but then, true performer that she was, began to play the melody in clear, bold, tones which complemented Brenneker's descant. Laurel played every variation, and Brenneker knew them all and answered back. The people in the audience were amazed that someone could play two-part harmony on one instrument. This was the most lovely duet arrangement of "The Ash Grove" that the judges had ever heard.

"That's the first time I ever heard anyone play a duet alone," said the young man with the lute as she came down from the stage. "Your harmony was better than any duet I've ever heard. How did you ever do that?"

Flustered, Laurel answered, "I don't know. I guess sometimes one must be alone to truly be in harmony with one's self."

A few more contestants got up to play, but they seemed half-hearted. The contest went of course to Laurel, who was almost as bewildered at her music as was everyone else. When she ascended the stage to accept the scholarship, the audience cheered and whistled for an encore.

Laurel sat down and prepared to play again, but just then there came a terrible wrenching sound and a loud snap. Brenneker saw the roof fly off her home, pulling a tangle of cobwebs after it. She cowered by the sound pegs, weak and frightened, and saw the face of Laurel staring down at her. Raising one timorous leg, she strummed a chord on her music web and thought she saw recognition in Laurel's eyes.

One of the judges came onstage to help pick up the debris. When he say the large spider, he said, "How ugly! Let me kill it for you."

"No," said Laurel. "It's the fairy harpist that Sanger told me about. See how she plays her web like a harp. She's been my secret friend all these years."

Because Brenneker appeared to be in a very weakened state and near death, Laurel kept her in a bottle for a few days and fed her all the crickets she could catch. Then, when it appeared that the spider would live, she took her back to the small town and turned her loose in the woods.

It was not the woods of home, but Brenneker found a hollow tree in which to string her harp and was quite content to play her songs alone for a while, although she missed Laurel's music. When spring came that next year, she played her love song to the open air, and it was Wisterness who came, tapping shyly on her web strings to attract her attention.

"I have always loved your songs," she said. "I had hoped you would come."

"Now you shall play my songs," he said, and he sacrificed himself to their mutual need.

Weeks later, she watched her young spiderlings float away on their kiteless strings, and she knew she would not play alone anymore. Then, feeling the deep harmony of the universe in her soul, she returned her web to the Dorian mode and played the gentle, lilting sadness that was now Wisterness.

# BUILDING A NEW FANTASY TRADITION

**The Unlikely Ones** by Mary Brown
Anne McCaffrey raved over *The Unlikely Ones*: "What a splendid, unusual and intriguing fantasy quest! You've got a winner here. . . ." Marion Zimmer Bradley called it "Really wonderful . . . I shall read and re-read this one." A traditional quest fantasy with quite an unconventional twist, we think you'll like it just as much as Anne McCaffrey and Marion Zimmer Bradley did.

**Knight of Ghosts and Shadows**
by Mercedes Lackey & Ellen Guon
Elves in L.A.? It would explain a lot, wouldn't it? In fact, half a millennium ago, when the elves were driven from Europe they came to—where else? —Southern California. Happy at first, they fell on hard times after one of their number tried to force the rest to be his vassals. Now it's up to one poor human to save them if he can. A knight in shining armor he's not, but he's one hell of a bard!

**The Interior Life** by Katherine Blake
Sue had three kids, one husband, a lovely home and a boring life. Sometimes, she just wanted to escape, to get out of her mundane world and *live* a little. So she did. And discovered that an active fantasy life can be a very dangerous thing—and very real. . . . Poul Anderson thought *The Interior Life* was "a breath of fresh air, bearing originality, exciting narrative, vividly realized characters— everything we have been waiting for for too long."

**The Shadow Gate** by Margaret Ball
The only good elf is a dead elf—or so the militant order of Durandine monks thought. And they planned on making sure that all the elves in their world (where an elvish Eleanor of Aquitaine ruled in Southern France) were very, very good. The elves of Three Realms have one last spell to bring help . . . and received it: in the form of the staff of the new Age Psychic Research Center of Austin, Texas. . . .

***Hawk's Flight*** by Carol Chase
Taverik, a young merchant, just wanted to be left alone to make an honest living. Small chance of that though: after their caravan is ambushed Taverik discovers that his best friend Marko is the last living descendant of the ancient Vos dynasty. The man who murdered Marko's parents still wants to wipe the slate clean—with Marko's blood. They try running away, but Taverik and Marko realize that there is a fate worse than death . . . That sooner or later, you have to stand and fight.

***A Bad Spell in Yurt*** by C. Dale Brittain
As a student in the wizards' college, young Daimbert had shown a distinct flair for getting himself in trouble. Now the newly appointed Royal Wizard to the backwater Kingdom of Yurt learns that his employer has been put under a fatal spell. Daimbert begins to realize that finding out who is responsible may require all the magic he'd never quite learned properly in the first place—with the kingdom's welfare and his life the price of failure. Good thing Daimbert knows how to improvise!

# PRAISE FOR
# LOIS MCMASTER BUJOLD

## What the critics say:

**The Warrior's Apprentice**: "Now here's a fun romp through the spaceways—not so much a space opera as space ballet.... it has all the 'right stuff.' A lot of thought and thoughtfulness stand behind the all-too-human characters. Enjoy this one, and look forward to the next."            —Dean Lambe, *SF Reviews*

"The pace is breathless, the characterization thoughtful and emotionally powerful, and the author's narrative technique and command of language compelling. Highly recommended."            —*Booklist*

**Brothers in Arms**: "... she gives it a geniune depth of character, while reveling in the wild turnings of her tale.... Bujold is as audacious as her favorite hero, and as brilliantly (if sneakily) successful."            —*Locus*

"Miles Vorkosigan is such a great character that I'll read anything Lois wants to write about him.... a book to re-read on cold rainy days." —Robert Coulson, *Comics Buyer's Guide*

**Borders of Infinity**: "Bujold's series hero Miles Vorkosigan may be a lord by birth and an admiral by rank, but a bone disease that has left him hobbled and in frequent pain has sensitized him to the suffering of outcasts in his very hierarchical era.... Playing off Miles's reserve and cleverness, Bujold draws outrageous and outlandish foils to color her high-minded adventures."            —*Publishers Weekly*

**Falling Free**: "In *Falling Free* Lois McMaster Bujold has written her fourth straight superb novel.... How to break down a talent like Bujold's into analyzable components? Best not to try. Best to say 'Read, or you will be missing something extraordinary.'" —Roland Green, *Chicago Sun-Times*

**The Vor Game**: "The chronicles of Miles Vorkosigan are far too witty to be literary junk food, but they rouse the kind of craving that makes popcorn magically vanish during a double feature."            —Faren Miller, *Locus*

# MORE PRAISE FOR
# LOIS MCMASTER BUJOLD

### What the readers say:

"My copy of *Shards of Honor* is falling apart I've reread it so often.... I'll read whatever you write. You've certainly proved yourself a grand storyteller."
—Liesl Kolbe, Colorado Springs, CO

"I experience the stories of Miles Vorkosigan as almost viscerally uplifting.... But certainly, even the weightiest theme would have less impact than a cinder on snow were it not for a rousing good story, and good storytelling with it. This is the second thing I want to thank you for.... I suppose if you boiled down all I've said to its simplest expression, it would be that I immensely enjoy and admire your work. I submit that, as literature, your work raises the overall level of the science fiction genre, and spiritually, your work cannot avoid positively influencing all who read it."
—Glen Stonebraker, Gaithersburg, MD

" 'The Mountains of Mourning' [in *Borders of Infinity*] was one of the best-crafted, and simply best, works I'd ever read. When I finished it, I immediately turned back to the beginning and read it again, and I can't remember the last time I did that."
—Betsy Bizot, Lisle, IL

"I can only hope that you will continue to write, so that I can continue to read (and of course buy) your books, for they make me laugh and cry and think ... rare indeed."
—Steven Knott, Major, USAF

# What do you say?

Send me these books!

*Shards of Honor* • 72087-2 • $4.99 \_\_\_\_\_
*The Warrior's Apprentice* • 72066-X • $4.50 \_\_\_\_\_
*Ethan of Athos* • 65604-X • $2.95 \_\_\_\_\_
*Falling Free* • 65398-9 • $4.99 \_\_\_\_\_
*Brothers in Arms* • 69799-4 • $3.95 \_\_\_\_\_
*Borders of Infinity* • 69841-9 • $4.99 \_\_\_\_\_
*The Vor Game* • 72014-7 • $4.50 \_\_\_\_\_
*Barrayar* • 72083-X • $4.99 \_\_\_\_\_

## Lois McMaster Bujold:
## Only from Baen Books

*If these books are not available at your local bookstore, just check your choices above, fill out this coupon and send a check or money order for the cover price to Baen Books, Dept. BA, P.O. Box 1403, Riverdale, NY 10471.*

NAME: _____

ADDRESS: _____

_____

I have enclosed a check or money order in the amount of $ _____.